TWO SPINSTERS AND A VILLAIN

TWO SPINSTERS AND A MURDER MYSTERY

EVE TARRINGTON

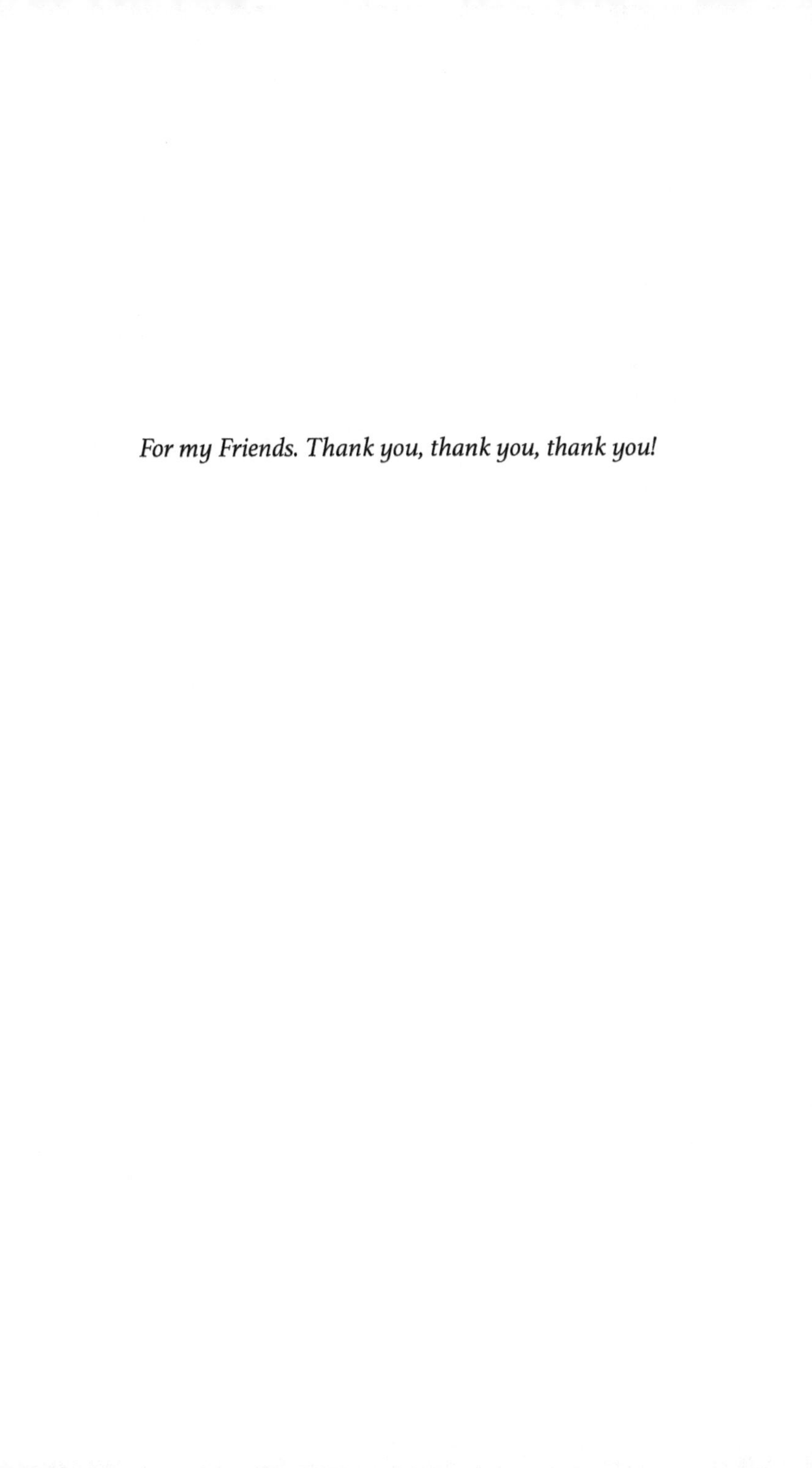

For my Friends. Thank you, thank you, thank you!

ALSO BY EVE TARRINGTON

Two Spinsters and a Corpse

Two Spinsters and a Duel

Two Spinsters and a Madman

Two Spinsters Books 1-3 Box Set

Two Spinsters and a Thief

Two Spinsters and an Assassin

Two Spinsters and a Swindler (Coming Soon)

1

———

Miss Angel Sweet, one of the prettiest actresses the Lyceum Theatre had ever seen, picked up a rock from the street and tossed it into the air. She caught it in her gloved hand without having to look up. All the while, she glared at her fellow actress, the buxom and beautiful Miss Theodosia Wynn.

"I ought to throw this stone at your head, *Miss* Wynn," said Miss Sweet, her high-pitched voice loud enough for the whole street to hear.

"You can't hit the high notes, little Angel, so I'm not sure why you think you can hit me," said Miss Wynn to the jeers of the crowd on the pavement.

Men, women, and children were quickly gathering. Though it was some time until the dress rehearsal for the new opera was due to begin, nobody could pass the two beautiful actresses without wishing to see which would best the other in a fight. After all, the dramatic quarrel outside the Lyceum Theatre might well end up surpassing anything the patrons would see later in the week.

Several yards away, a trio of observers watched the two

actresses trade vicious, elegant insults. Mr Ivo Solier, a French composer, frowned and looked away. Miss Judith St Clair, his friend, knew that poor Mr Solier would not be interested in what the two young women were saying. He only wished to steal a few minutes with the theatre's director before the start of the rehearsal because he felt sure that he could convince her to accept his little comic opera if she were only to hear parts of it played aloud.

The third person in the trio was the only one who relished a good battle. Miss Louisa-Margaretta Haddington was Mr Solier's fiancée, and she was plainly enjoying herself.

"Both Miss Wynn and Miss Sweet have been lovers of the Duke of Ormonde," she breathed. "So naturally, they hate each other. That red hair! You must admit the duke likes a certain type of lady."

Though Judith was well used to hearing such scandalous statements from her irreverent friend, she could not keep from blushing. She wished that Louisa-Margaretta would not repeat such indecent gossip in the company of a gentleman. It was most embarrassing for all concerned. "Louisa-Margaretta, you must not say such things."

Privately, Judith did not agree with her friend when it came to the Duke of Ormonde's taste in women, though she would never say so aloud. Miss Angel Sweet looked like the perfect personification of her name. Her pale skin was milky, her little red ringlets almost childlike, though her face was that of a woman. Judith's cousin, Jasper St Clair, worked with Miss Angel Sweet and had said that she was twenty years old. Popular opinion put Miss Sweet's age nearer sixteen, and of course, the lady herself only giggled and batted her eyelashes when asked.

Miss Wynn, who was rolling her eyes as she mocked

Miss Sweet's sorry dancing, looked very different. She was taller, with a figure that was much fuller and healthier. Her skin was olive, her hair a deep shade of red with looser curls. Though Judith had asked him, Jasper had not told her Miss Wynn's age, murmuring that he did not know her well. But Judith was certain that Miss Wynn must be a good bit older than Miss Sweet.

"Should we try to calm them?" asked Judith, hoping that Louisa-Margaretta would tell her not to intervene. Though Judith had managed her share of disagreements, the way Miss Wynn and Miss Sweet were carrying on was foreign to her. As accomplished opera singers, both had voices that would carry for miles. Neither had specifically mentioned the Duke of Ormonde in their present argument, but Judith imagined this was only due to some remaining shred of delicacy, for the gossip that the two had been the duke's lovers had spread across London. One of the women near Judith was loudly speculating that the duke might marry Miss Sweet, and Miss Wynn would be angry that he had thrown her over.

"We should go," said Mr Solier in French, sounding as bored as he had during their long journey from St Petersburg. The whole time they were on the ship, he speculated about his chances of getting one of his operas performed in London. Yet since their arrival, in spite of their combined efforts, he had not yet succeeded.

Judith and Louisa-Margaretta both turned to look at the composer. When they did, they missed the moment when Miss Sweet threw herself on Miss Wynn. When Judith looked again, the smaller woman was on top of the other one's back. Miss Sweet had one arm around Miss Wynn's neck, the other fist in her hair. Miss Wynn was screaming, both her hands locked around Miss Sweet's fist.

Louisa-Margaretta ran over. "Ladies!" she said. "Surely you must save your beautiful voices."

Judith followed, fearing that Louisa-Margaretta would be injured.

But Miss Sweet only dropped down from the other lady's back, glaring at her. "And who might you be? I have business with this woman."

Judith hurried forward, putting a gentle hand on Louisa-Margaretta's arm. "We are the guests of your fellow actor, Mr Jasper St Clair," she said, trying to speak softly. But the crowd had gone quiet, so she was sure they must be able to hear her every word.

"Welcome," said Miss Wynn, her smile so open and seemingly sincere that Judith found herself unnerved. "Let me show you to your friend. I'm sure he shall be pleased to see you."

Mr Solier hurried forward, happy to be entering the theatre and not at all bothered by the onlookers' stares.

"I haven't finished with you," said Miss Wynn, her face growing cold as she looked at Miss Sweet again.

The latter folded her arms and glared.

Judith blushed in embarrassment, wishing they had chosen a different time to visit the theatre. It appeared that there were just as many dramatics off the stage as on it, and it was very discomfiting.

2

———

Louisa-Margaretta only half followed the conversation as Miss Wynn took them to the green room, where the other actors were waiting. The opera was a small one, so there were only three men and three women. The third woman, in contrast to the two fiery ones who had been fighting on the street, was sitting on a sofa, reading a book of poetry. An older gentleman squeezed Miss Wynn's arm with some familiarity. He was the only other person, and Judith said she was not sure whether Jasper had yet arrived.

Miss Wynn's face broke into a smile as she saw the man. "Might you fetch Mr St Clair for us? He has visitors."

"Yes," said the man. "And after that, you are to go down and consult on the fabric for one of the gowns."

She sighed. "I should much rather not, Mr Daw."

"Mustn't dawdle, my dear," he said. "Though I know you have a great many responsibilities."

Miss Wynn frowned. "I wish my duties could begin and end with the stage, I must say."

He gave her a wink. "They never have and never will,

dearest Theodosia. But take heart! We'll have quite an audience tonight, though we all know it is only a rehearsal, eh?"

He gave a warm smile to the group and touched his hat as he left the room. He returned with Jasper.

Miss Wynn stood by the door as if she were about to leave, but Judith noticed she was observing the way Jasper greeted the newcomers.

"Well, well," Jasper said in sloppy French. Judith's cousin had always been handsome but never more so than at the theatre. He was wearing a roguish costume, all sharp cuts of fabric and red silk, perfect for his comedic role. He kissed the ladies' hands and embraced Mr Solier. "Miss Haddington, *mon chere monsieur*. Dearest Judith. How strange it is to see all of you in this room!"

"Is the director ready to see us?" asked Mr Solier in French. Though they had been in England for two days, he had yet to speak a word of English. He simply spoke French to everyone, trusting that most would understand enough to help him.

"If it's a difficult evening, we could return another day," said Judith, looking at Miss Wynn with doubt in her eyes.

Louisa-Margaretta had to suppress a smile. Poor Judith had been unsettled by the fight outside the theatre and was no doubt hoping they could leave the little theatre entirely. To Louisa-Margaretta, the conflict between the two ladies had been exhilarating. She had been raised in a world where it was a great scandal if two ladies so much as raised their voices. When she'd pulled Miss Sweet off Miss Wynn, she could feel how angry both women were that they had not been given the chance to finish their fight.

Jasper shook his head. "We're still waiting to get the final version from those wicked censors, so who knows what we shall be singing on opening night. But in the meantime, this dress rehearsal is meant to raise a few funds. At least enough to hire another actor and actress in case one of us falls ill before a performance. Nothing happens in the theatre without money!"

Ivo Solier huffed. "That is very true," he said. "And it seems you English have little appreciation for opera."

"Don't scold Judith's cousin. He is our best hope," snapped Louisa-Margaretta, but Jasper only laughed.

"We're all in need of a laugh now that we are at war once again. And you're quite fortunate to have come to the best opera house in London! Come now. I'll show you to the people in charge," Jasper said.

3

Mr Solier was hot on Jasper's heels as he took them to a small room. A woman in trousers was stooped over a chest, rummaging through dresses. Louisa-Margaretta took her for the wardrobe mistress.

"We need the director," she said to Jasper, her smile dancing between politeness and impatience. Surely, Judith's cousin should not be so silly as to imagine that the well-known French composer could be fobbed off on some little underling.

The lithe woman rose to her feet, nodding to the assembled party.

Jasper made the introductions. "Miss Byrd, may I present Mr Ivo Solier, Miss St Clair, and Miss Haddington. This is Miss Byrd, our fearless director."

Clearly, he'd said in in jest, for the woman looked anything but fearless. She was clenching her hands with the effort of pausing in her labors. "Thank you. Very nice to meet you all. I trust our Mr St Clair will show you about."

She turned again to the chest, leaving the dresses she had pulled out on the floor.

"Here," said Judith, lowering herself so that she was next to the director. "May I help you find something?"

"Yes," said the woman sharply. "Fiordiligi needs a proper dress for the second act, something with a bit of silk and color. This pale muslin is the most pathetic thing I have ever seen, yet everything we have is as dull as ditchwater."

Louisa-Margaretta sighed at the woman's strident tone, but Judith was accustomed to acceding to unreasonable requests and did not hesitate. "Of course," she murmured. "I'm sure we can find something suitable."

"I am not," said the director, rising to her feet and opening another chest. "I'm not sure why we called this a dress rehearsal. Nobody will be dressed properly at all."

"Ah, but we shall sound beautiful," said Jasper. "Really, Miss Byrd, this is an excellent production. And it would be even better with the addition of a comic opera by this esteemed gentleman here."

Miss Byrd's eyes widened with shock. "No, of course not. There is no money at all for such a thing. You must see that this is not possible."

"I do not see," began Louisa-Margaretta. But before she could try to summon a spirited defense of her fiancé's work, they were interrupted.

A dark, handsome, exceedingly well-dressed man came through the door. His looks had been called "exotic" by many thanks to Chinese roots on one side of the family, but Louisa-Margaretta knew that he was every inch an English gentleman—and therefore not to be trusted.

"Ah, Miss St Clair, Miss Haddington," said Mr Fortescue. "And Mr St Clair! I was wondering if you happened to be a relation."

Mr St Clair did not answer but appeared calm as he introduced Mr Fortescue and Mr Solier. At the word *intended*, Mr Fortescue's eyebrows shot up.

"Oh, how lovely," he said. "Miss Haddington, I wish you every happiness in marriage. Mr Solier, congratulations."

"Thank you," said Mr Solier without any real interest. Louisa-Margaretta did not bother responding. She knew that Mr Fortescue was hoping she would be happy in marriage—to himself, not to another.

Mr Fortescue's smile was handsome, but it had wolfish undertones. If only Louisa-Margaretta had seen those from the first. His intelligence and wit, however, had kept her from thinking clearly.

When Louisa-Margaretta was staying with a friend in London, she had been captivated by Mr Fortescue. He was one of the few people willing to have real conversations with her, beyond the constrictions of politeness, and he seemed to see her spinsterhood as something of a personal challenge. His attempt at seduction might not have been enough to endanger Louisa-Margaretta's virtue, but she had allowed him to see her alone, without a chaperone, and in her infatuation had kissed him more than once. He could ruin her reputation by lying about those encounters, thereby forcing her to marry him.

Though Louisa-Margaretta had naturally begged Mr Fortescue not to make good on his threat to ruin her, he held fast to the condition that they must marry. All the things that put off other gentlemen, such as Louisa-Margaretta's sharp tongue and her impatience with social convention, only served to make her more enticing to Mr Fortescue. She had hoped to escape him by leaving the country, but it seemed he would never forget what had passed between them.

"Your little coterie is welcome here, as usual," said Miss Byrd. What little politeness she had forced into her voice sounded most unnatural indeed. She was a poor actress, so perhaps it was just as well that she was directing, though Louisa-Margaretta had certainly never heard of a woman being given such a role.

"Yes," said Mr Fortescue. "But when I learned my *dear* friends were in town, I had to see them! What brings you to this theatre?"

Louisa-Margaretta moved to stop her fiancé, but he was smiling and shameless. The animation that had deserted him when the director refused to listen to his idea returned as he spoke to a well-dressed, obviously wealthy gentleman.

"This opera needs a short comic opera as well," he said, laboring over the consonants so he would be understood perfectly. "I have one that would serve the theatre very well, but I'm told they have no money."

Mr Fortescue's grin grew broader. He looked exactly as if he were going to find a torch and set fire to the entire theatre. It was enough to make Louisa-Margaretta both scared and angry, but Mr Solier seemed impervious to the danger.

"Ah, if it is a question of money!" he said. "Dear Miss Byrd, I would be happy to pay for two weeks of the opera's run, provided you add this small comic piece. After all, it is expected, and your production will be very short without something of this nature."

Miss Byrd blinked. But to her credit, she recovered quickly. "Very well," she said. "Mr Solier, you may leave your opera, though its acceptance shall depend on how it fares with the censors. I am still waiting for the final word on this opera as well. I have a feeling Mr Mozart's liberality may not sit so well with some of the gentlemen in that office."

She sniffed, and Louisa-Margaretta was unable to tell whether she approved more of Mr Mozart or of the "English sensibilities" he might offend. Perhaps Miss Byrd did not wish others to know her true opinion on the subject.

"Excellent," said Mr Fortescue. "You may send me all the papers, but I'm sure we shall have no trouble at all.

"No," said Louisa-Margaretta far too late, looking between the parties. As a rule, she rarely felt frantic, but she knew that being in Mr Fortescue's debt would only end poorly for all involved.

"My dear," said Mr Solier. It was a phrase he only used in annoyance.

"Of course, it is quite possible that another theatre will take this up, but none has accepted it, unless my information was incorrect?" Mr Fortescue asked in perfect French.

Louisa-Margaretta shifted in embarrassment. She had felt from the first that Mr Fortescue already knew of her engagement, and now, he was proving this to be true. Somehow, from the moment they'd set foot in London, he had most likely followed all of their movements. And he had encountered them in the Lyceum Theatre, claiming that it was a fortunate chance meeting. Louisa-Margaretta was not fooled.

Mr Solier was not at all ashamed of his comic opera's poor reception, however, and he chattered on. "Indeed not," he said, plainly happy to be speaking French. "The theatres here, they are centuries behind! One would think they are against all art. They hesitate so at every single joke—"

"Yes, the London artistic world is remarkably unsophisticated," remarked Mr Fortescue.

Miss Byrd sniffed. "Well, we are going to bring the sophistication," she said.

Judith silently passed a long orange gown into Miss

Byrd's hands, and the latter sniffed. "Yes, this will do nicely. Any of you who wish to watch from the wings may stay, but I must ask that you vacate this area. Our actors can tolerate no distraction tonight, I'm afraid."

Mr Fortescue, still grinning, slipped out before Louisa-Margaretta could confront him. She left with a worried Judith and a buoyant Mr Solier. After Jasper left them, Louisa-Margaretta dragged both parties out of the area and took them to a box. Since the audience was relatively small, consisting only of people who were known to the theatre and wished to make a donation in order to view one of the final rehearsals, they might as well enjoy some of the best seats.

"Let us hope the show is worth all this trouble," she grumbled. "From what I've seen, none of these actors is likely to put a damper on their own feelings for long enough to convince us we're in another world."

Fortunately, she was very much mistaken.

4

———————

Judith had already heard enough about Mr Mozart's *Così fan tutte* to be familiar with the premise. Miss Wynn was playing Fiordiligi, the beautiful woman betrothed to Jasper's Guglielmo. Miss Sweet was Dorabella, Fiordiligi's sister, betrothed to Mr Nightingale's Ferrando. She watched as Mr Daw, transformed into the devious character Don Alfonso, urged the young men to believe that their fiancées would not be faithful.

Louisa-Margaretta looked over at Judith then turned back to the stage without saying anything. She often spoke without thinking, so Judith was troubled by her silence. And she bristled. *How could anyone see my story—and dear Morgan's—in this silly little opera?* He believed that she would stay faithful to him, and he was correct. She did not doubt that he retained the same devotion.

Judith and Louisa-Margaretta's cousin, Mr Morgan Ramsbury, had long had an understanding. They'd announced their formal engagement to Judith's family before the trip to Russia, though the news was not particularly welcome. Judith's father was a rector in the Church of

England, and Morgan was a Quaker. Still, Judith hoped that a lengthy engagement would give her father and sister time to accept the unconventional match.

But the trip to Russia had not gone to plan. Morgan, moved by a genuine desire to see the countries of Europe divided in a fair and just manner, had gotten a minor position with an English diplomat and gone to join the Congress of Vienna. But by Christmas, he was declared missing. He and two other men had left, and somewhere in France, they vanished. Since then, for a torturous six months, there had been no word.

Judith was usually too worried for Morgan's well-being to remember her unease about his fidelity. Sometimes, the whispers about the Viscount Rialton affected her more than she let on. *Could Morgan have been influenced by that man and his famous appetites?* In the daylight, before God, she was certain that he was incorruptible. Yet that man's company along with all the rumoured debauchery of the Congress of Vienna made her wonder. After all, apparently, the monarchs had been having such a lovely time that they had not even prevented Napoleon Bonaparte from rising once more.

Judith attempted to keep her attention on the stage, where the characters of Fiordiligi and Dorabella were singing about how they loved their fiancés. The women were marvelous actresses, as their glances and embraces told only of the most devoted sisterhood. Nobody would have believed that they had been in front of the theatre only an hour earlier, threatening to kill each other. Indeed, Miss Wynn was a particularly compelling Fiordiligi. When Jasper entered as Guglielmo, the tender embraces he shared with her were so emphatic that Judith found herself looking away.

"Oh, Judith," said Louisa-Margaretta. "Is this opera too scandalous for your liking? Should we have seen something tragic instead?"

"I agree," said Mr Solier, not understanding the statement. "It is trash! The libretto sounds very ill, and nothing about the music saves it."

Judith shook her head. "There is nothing wrong with it, though I confess I don't understand every word."

She looked at the stage again, still a bit uncomfortable at the sight of Fiordiligi clasped tight in Guglielmo's embrace. The other pair, she noticed, did not embrace as much. Mr Nightingale turned toward Miss Sweet every so often, but as soon as he had a line to sing, he faced the audience again and turned his face toward the boxes. Perhaps, having been told his whole life that he was exceedingly handsome, he felt the need to display his striking visage. And Miss Sweet seemed unable to keep an impish smile from creeping across her features occasionally, though she quickly schooled them back into a lovelorn but beautiful frown.

"They are very skilled," murmured Judith to Louisa-Margaretta. "I'm surprised that none of them has a role at a larger theatre."

Louisa-Margaretta shook her head. "Then you have not spent enough time in London theatres, Judith. There are few enough roles for opera singers, and those that do exist tend to go to famous people like Mrs Bartleby. Though I do wonder why Mr and Mrs Daw are acting here. They are both famous enough to have gotten better parts."

"That, I can explain," said Judith. "According to Jasper, both Miss Sweet and Miss Wynn are protégés of the Daws. Though the younger ladies despise each other, Mr and Mrs Daw are devoted to each of them. I am sure they hope to help their stars rise."

"Well," said Louisa-Margaretta, "I hope that may come true. For I would come to this theatre just to see Mrs Daw. I believe Despina is supposed to be a young girl, but Mrs Daw plays her perfectly in spite of being at least thirty years too old for the role."

Judith tried to lose her troubles in admiring Mrs Daw's performance. But thoughts of Morgan weighed on her heart, and she spent the rest of the act twisting her handkerchief, hoping that she would be able to keep tears at bay.

5

The first intermission came before Louisa-Margaretta would have wished. She had been so enjoying the opera that she felt as if it might last forever. But during the interval, she had to straighten her posture then go down in search of some sort of beverage for Judith, who was feeling ill.

"I can get it myself," said Judith, her face pale.

Louisa-Margaretta shook her head. "Don't be a fool. Sit. I won't be a moment."

But she dawdled on the stairs, admiring the theatre's beautiful decorations—the way the chandeliers glistened, the intricacy of the murals. And though Jasper had little by way of financial resources, she envied him this life—the evenings filled with the sort of music that made her heart soar, the clearly marked chapters of his life. Louisa-Margaretta had some rather impressive memories that she had made during her time away from Derbyshire and London, but the rest of her days seemed a terrible muddle of drawing rooms and dancing.

"It's quite a superb little theatre, isn't it?" asked Mr Fortescue.

Louisa-Margaretta's mouth tightened. She did not wish to say anything to him, but she gave a false smile in case one of the people milling about should notice her silence.

She had not noticed him approach her, but knowing the man, she was sure he would not have strayed far. He had a knack for interrupting where his presence was not desired.

"You're so young," he continued. "And you look so lovely tonight, Miss Haddington."

Louisa-Margaretta gave a rather unladylike snort. She would never understand why men thought it was a compliment to tell a woman that she was young, as if she were a racehorse or a dog bred for hunting. And besides, she was not so very young for an unmarried lady, though she was certainly younger than Mr Fortescue.

"I must return to my seat," she said stiffly.

"And you must break off your engagement with Mr Solier," said Mr Fortescue. "Best to do it tonight, don't you think? Never fear. I will pay for his little comic opera, and he is more interested in his work than he is in you."

For a moment, Louisa-Margaretta was speechless, and Mr Fortescue took full advantage of her silence.

"Not that he is correct in this, of course," he said with false gallantry. "Anyone who would throw over such a jewel as you is certainly mad! Alas, I am told that great composers were ever thus."

"Well," said Louisa-Margaretta, "your thoughts are of little interest to me, Mr Fortescue. But I'm glad you have made a study of famous composers and their little whims. Thank you for telling me such interesting stories."

His expression darkened. "I have told you only this.

Unless you marry me, I will tell the entire world your family's sordid secrets. Not to mention something deliciously scandalous about your friend Miss St Clair. Of course, she is a—"

"Do not even think of it," said Louisa-Margaretta, aware that her voice was too loud but unable to speak softly. "Why would you threaten me with this nonsense once again? You said all that two years ago!"

"And you thought a little time at that lovely Wycliff Castle then a trip abroad would be enough to make me have a change of heart," said Mr Fortescue, a grin overtaking his features. "Oh, you fickle creature! You understand why I have not been able to give up on a woman of such beauty and spirit."

Louisa-Margaretta would have worn any silly costume, would have thrown a veil over her face every day of the year if she thought it would put Mr Fortescue off. But he was rich, and she knew very well that he loved nothing more than provoking the few women who had the courage to defy him. Or the one woman who did so, rather, for Louisa-Margaretta knew of no others. She was aware of plenty of mamas in London eager to keep Mr Fortescue away from their daughters, but because of his wealth and consequence, those ladies were all polite to his face.

Louisa-Margaretta was the opposite of polite.

"You repulsed me then, and I certainly would not think of spending a few moments with you now, let alone putting my freedom in your hands for the rest of my natural life," she said. "If you deluded yourself into thinking I would ever change my mind, you have only yourself to blame for that."

Mr Fortescue frowned. "You think I am making an idle threat."

"I think that I shall never marry you," said Louisa-

Margaretta. "And if you make good on these threats, I shall have you arrested for blackmail."

Mr Fortescue's frown was quickly replaced by a little smile. "Oh, I don't think that would be possible."

"The magistrate is an old friend of my family's," said Louisa-Margaretta. "In fact, I think I shall visit him while I'm in London."

She generally tried to avoid the magistrate, Mr Christmas Fudge, a man she respected but did not enjoy conversing with. But by all means, she would let Mr Fortescue think they were in constant contact.

Mr Fortescue withdrew as if surprised. "A magistrate will come arrest me merely for admiring your beauty and informing you of some very disturbing rumours that have reached my ears?" he said. "That is shocking indeed."

"I am going to marry Mr Solier," said Louisa-Margaretta, feeling quite sure of her decision for the very first time. "You cannot stop me."

"Oh, my dear," said Mr Fortescue. "Such a thing is impossible. The two of you are not at all well suited, and I would be remiss if I did not try to prevent such an ill-fated match."

Louisa-Margaretta stood perfectly still, trying not to move under Mr Fortescue's unflinching gaze. As usual, he had gotten rather near the truth. She and Mr Solier were not a perfect couple, and that had been clear from the first.

But it would be better than marrying a blackmailer.

"I will find a way to marry him or die trying," said Louisa-Margaretta.

"Careful," said Mr Fortescue. "Or you'll sound like a tragic opera heroine."

Louisa-Margaretta couldn't speak as he walked away, though she cursed him in her mind.

After he had left, the little orchestra started up again, and she whispered a promise. "I am not going to be any sort of tragic heroine. You villain, nothing about my life is tragic in the least."

And head held high, she went back into the box, where Judith and Mr Solier awaited her.

6

───────────

Judith had no interest in returning to the green room after the performance, but Mr Solier insisted.

"I must talk to that Miss Byrd, the director," said Mr Solier. "She will need copies of all of the music and libretto. I am not sure that the soprano or the mezzo soprano is quite loud enough to sing these roles."

Louisa-Margaretta shook her head. "Monsieur Solier, my dear," she said, though the words sounded hollow. "They are the only two ladies in all of London who may be willing to sing the roles, which is rather more to the point."

He glared at her. "My dear," he said, words that sounded just as hollow from his lips as they had from Louisa-Margaretta's a moment ago. "You have tried to sing these roles yourself and sung them rather well, though of course not with the strong voice we might expect from a professional. If Mademoiselle Wynn and Mademoiselle Sweet are not quite suited, we may as well put you on the stage."

Judith gasped in horror, and Louisa-Margaretta and Mr Solier both laughed.

"Your face, Judith!" said Louisa-Margaretta. "I know my

reputation is far from untarnished, but I haven't sunk quite so low as that."

As she said it, she cast a glance at the stage, and her smile wavered. Judith knew that her friend was hardly untroubled by her prospects. Louisa-Margaretta had never been satisfied with the life of a grand lady, though she did appreciate the idea of hunting or riding daily. She had been at her most satisfied when she and Judith were working, but if she were to return to that life, she would be risking her family's displeasure. Any sort of toil for material gain was considered dishonourable for a lady in her position unless it were concerned with charity or marriage.

Judith wondered if Louisa-Margaretta's dissatisfaction with her penniless, powerless state was pushing her toward the latter and wished she could explain to her friend that trading one form of drudgery for another was not necessarily wise—especially not marriage to a man such as Mr Solier, who was now scolding them to hurry.

"We must arrange everything, and this theatre is so small," he complained, shepherding them down the stairs and toward the door that led to the backstage area. "It is not where I would have wished to have my music introduced to a London audience."

Louisa-Margaretta sighed, shaking her head. Though Judith's own engagement had been fraught so far, she still remembered the early days when it was a complete secret from everyone—except, that was, from Louisa-Margaretta. *The stolen kisses, the dreams of hope fulfilled!* Judith had been so besotted with Morgan that she could not keep herself from bursting into foolish smiles, and she had to school her features carefully when in company. Louisa-Margaretta did not have any moments like that. Instead, finding the penniless but highly accomplished Mr Solier had come as the sort of good luck that one tried to appreciate, like a much-needed clean chamber pot during a vile illness or a tough, bland piece of meat during a time of deprivation.

"This is horrible news," said Miss Byrd, tears coming to her eyes as she paced the room.

The six cast members were gathered before her. Mr and Mrs Daw stood together, their faces sympathetic but not panicked. Miss Wynn, however, looked tearful, Miss Sweet angry. Jasper and Mr Nightingale both appeared confused.

Mr Daw patted the director on the shoulder. "It is one opera of many, my dear," he said. "We have but to choose another."

Mr Solier was completely without shame. He must have understood enough of the English to address the company in French.

"I could, of course, present you with another one of my works," he said. "You could perform it as the main attraction alongside my comic opera. It would, of course, be acceptable to your censors."

"This was not acceptable?" Judith softly asked her cousin.

Jasper shook his head. He swallowed several times before answering. "They've sent back the libretto many weeks late," he said. "That idiot George Coleman! He has cut so many sections that we scarcely have an opera left."

"I am sure there is a way," said Mrs Daw, appearing just as calm as her husband. "We can simply sing the things they have left."

The director brandished the papers over her head. "They make no sense!" she cried. "Nobody will come see us. They shall not be able to follow any part of the plot. Mr Coleman will not even allow us to have soldiers in the production!"

"We can tell the stories with our gestures," said Miss Sweet, her face becoming less flushed as she pondered the challenge. "That's what we're supposed to be doing anyway."

After a pause, Miss Wynn snapped to attention. "You ought to learn to do it, then," she jeered. She looked over at Louisa-Margaretta, Judith, and Mr Solier.

Judith, feeling awkward once again, ventured a suggestion. "How long would it take Mr Coleman to review it if you were to make more changes?"

"I wouldn't know how to change this," said the director. "I can't write libretto or music! I can sing a very little bit, and I can direct. Otherwise, I would write my own silly opera, one with no substance at all, and *that* would please that Mr Coleman!"

Mrs Daw was quick to catch Judith's meaning. "I forgot that we had a composer in our midst," she said. "Now that we have secured funding for his opera, perhaps Mr Solier would help us to revise this one."

The director took out a handkerchief, sighing as she wiped her eyes. "If we present Mr Coleman with a revised opera, he would get to it quickly, I know," she said. "He came very near apologizing for the delay with this opera, which is most unlike him. I believe he has been most unwell, and of course the war changed his task quite a bit."

Half a dozen pairs of pleading eyes were now fixed on Mr Solier but in vain.

"Wolfgang Amadeus Mozart," he said, the name sounding funny with his distinctly French pronunciation. "The fellow wouldn't know a decent opera if he were cast in one himself. I am sorry, but I do not work on such refuse."

"Even if it means your own opera doesn't premiere in London?" asked Louisa-Margaretta, touching his arm.

He patted her back with a sigh. "My dear, how little you understand of my art!"

They were all silent for several moments. The actors, giving up, began to murmur among themselves.

"We could do it," said Louisa-Margaretta quickly. "Miss St Clair and I."

"Could you?" asked Mr Daw warmly. "What talent we have in our midst!"

"No," said Judith. "You're about to be married, and I have other business in London! Truly, we could not."

"Dear Miss St Clair is a genius with music," said Louisa-Margaretta. "And I'm quite sure she does not feel that helping her cousin is beneath her. Dear Mr St Clair, after you have been such an excellent host to us, how could we refuse to help?"

Mr Solier was still unconvinced. "Perhaps this Mr Coleman noticed that the opera was of poor quality," he said. "And if it were torn to pieces and rewritten, I am afraid that could not solve any of the problems."

Glaring at Mr Solier, Louisa-Margaretta went on. "I am rather good with libretto myself, and I'm sure I could write the music quickly enough with my friend's help."

It was not a vain boast. Louisa-Margaretta had such an excellent memory for libretto that she might well be able to sing at least half the opera having listened to it only once, and it would be child's play for her to rewrite the words to suit Mr Coleman's criticisms.

"That would be wonderful," said Miss Wynn. "And there are some sections where the range is, I confess, rather high for a mezzo soprano. Could you help us there?"

Judith shook her head, but Louisa-Margaretta smiled. "Of course we could! I shall leave all that to Judith. She can manage the music quite well."

"Of course," said Miss Wynn. "Please, Miss St Clair. After all, you have the ability to write your own music, and this would not be nearly as taxing as true composition. It is only rewriting. I'm sure you would find it simple."

Judith sighed. "I cannot promise that we will end up with an opera that satisfies all of you."

Mr Daw laughed heartily. "My dear Miss St Clair, think nothing of that! We wish only to perform for an audience. Whether an opera is satisfactory or not means shockingly little when one has to eat."

Mr Solier's nose was distinctly wrinkled at that. "If you are an artist, can it be said that you hold the nature of your art in no esteem at all?"

"I don't intend to be a starving artist, sir, and that's the difference. In your case, I imagine your hosts are feeding you rather well!"

Mr Solier made no response, though Judith felt certain he had understood. She knew that Mr Solier's haughty bearing hid a measure of shame. In France, he had been an aristocrat, but since his exile, he was merely another person dependent on the goodwill of others. If he were to marry Louisa-Margaretta, her fortune would be his, and the success or failure of his operas would not be the only thing he could rely on for material comfort.

Of course, composing only operatic music was not an easy way to earn a living. In fact, Judith had already suggested that Mr Solier try his hand at writing popular songs. Morgan had once given her the same advice. But he had refused to consider it, saying he would rather earn a wage digging ditches if he had to. He said it with the perfect certainly of one who has never needed to dirty his hands, even in exile.

"It is settled, then," said Louisa-Margaretta. "We shall fix it all in good time, and you may open the production on the original schedule if you wish."

"And if the manuscript comes back by then, and if Mr Coleman is pleased with our revisions," Judith hastened to add, but she got no response.

The older couple had begun to lead the assembled in an aria of thanksgiving, something from another opera, which sounded beautiful and jubilant coming from the whole company—and, it must be said, impressively loud. She did not agree at all with Mr Solier that Miss Sweet and Miss Wynn had voices that were lacking. Miss Sweet's voice was not as well-trained as Miss Wynn's. That much was true. Sometimes, there was ornamentation in her singing that seemed to belong more to a folk melody than an elegant work of art. But little Angel Sweet was very young, and Judith was certain she would gain the precision of Miss Wynn's vocals in time.

They were interrupted by the entrance of a rather good-looking man dressed in the finest clothing that Judith had ever seen. Though Louisa-Margaretta's parents had entertained many guests at Wycliff Castle, both those with royal blood and those with a great deal of money, the man appeared better dressed than all of them. And his countenance, while rather overwhelmingly jolly, was pleasing.

"I've come to bring my little lady home!" he said. "Our carriage awaits in the front, dear one."

He did not need to announce himself as the duke who had taken up with Miss Sweet. Judith could hardly believe the innocent expression on that lady's face as she strode over to the man, taking his arm with affection that seemed perfectly genuine. She appeared more at ease with him than she had with either Jasper or Mr Nightingale on the stage, though he was two decades her senior.

Judith looked away. She could not bear even to look at Miss Wynn, who had started to say something then apparently thought the better of it. She feared a repeat of the scene that had happened earlier, but fortunately, the duke whisked his companion away very quickly. Miss Wynn, even if she had objected, had no time to resort to fisticuffs.

Louisa-Margaretta squeezed Judith's hand, looking gleeful. "Oh, don't be such an old woman, Judith," she said. "It's not unheard of for pretty actresses to have admirers, you know."

Judith did not say anything, but her cheeks burned. Louisa-Margaretta would not understand her sensibilities. She did not find it shocking that men and women had relations outside of marriage. Indeed, she had been privy to that information from a young age, probably before Louisa-Margaretta had even learned of it. As the daughter of a clergyman, she often saw her mother provide for young women who were with child. She knew very well how often marriages were rushed as well as how easily the strictures of courtship fell away as soon as the banns were read, before the wedding itself.

But it was the shamelessness of the thing that shocked her. *Miss Sweet's happy and innocent face!* For the same reason, the embraces between Jasper and Miss Wynn onstage had embarrassed her. It was not as if she believed nobody ever embraced, and indeed, when she was with Morgan in happier times, she had been rather shameless in seeking out time alone with him. But on a stage was a different thing. Seeing her cousin in such a brazen profession as acting, where one might pretend to make passionate —but convincing—love to a lady in front of dozens of onlookers was distinctly odd.

"I'm not being fussy," said Judith. "I'm only tired. We

ought to go home and sleep if we are to spend tomorrow rewriting an entire opera."

Louisa-Margaretta gave a musical laugh. "Oh, it won't be so much trouble! Don't you wish to save the whole company?"

The actors were speaking among themselves, and Mr Nightingale was playing an aria from another work on the old pianoforte that stood in the corner.

"This won't be a balm for all our troubles," said Judith quietly once she was quite sure that nobody was listening to their conversation. "What of Mr Fortescue?"

Louisa-Margaretta's expression darkened as she stood. "The opera first," she said. "Once that goes back to Mr Coleman, we can think of something suitable for that villain."

"We cannot let him continue to have a hold over us," said Judith after looking around at the actors, who had broken into a loud debate about the merits of *castrati* as soon as Mr Nightingale finished playing the aria. Apparently, they were rarely quiet, even when they did not need to sing.

Louisa-Margaretta nodded solemnly. "Do not trouble yourself, Judith," she said. "I shall think of something."

7

———

Judith was the only person who joined Cousin Dorothy at breakfast.

"I hope you didn't hear too much of an ill report from your brother last night," she said by way of conversation.

Dorothy's green eyes widened. "I heard nothing," she said.

Judith gave a little laugh. "I imagine he returned home rather late, then."

Dorothy's eyes went to Jasper's bedroom then back to Judith. "We never eat breakfast this early," she said with some regret. "It is a great relief finding someone with whom I may pass the time."

Judith started. "But you have many friends in London, surely!"

Dorothy gave a tight smile. "Yes. Well. They have all married and are quite occupied with their own families."

"I see," said Judith, then she took a bite of her crumpet.

Dorothy had not yet begun eating. "I am not sure you do see," she said. "I remember when we were girls, you were so surprised that I wished to get into Almack's and find a husband. I was ready to pick the locks if I could, and you wanted to avoid ballrooms entirely."

Judith coloured. She did remember one visit, during which she had begged her mother to put off her entrance into society until a later year. Dorothy, on the other hand, was well prepared to rush into marriage.

"I'm sure I only thought one must be cautious," Judith said. "An alliance before God and for life?"

Dorothy gave a harsh laugh. "Yes, if only marriages could be like national alliances! We are friends with France then sworn enemies then friends demanding concessions. And now we are enemies again, and they may kill us in our beds if they wish."

Judith looked at her plate. Her father would say to put one's faith in God. But that wasn't terribly encouraging when one was aware of the slaughter for which Napoleon was responsible. The most one could do was to believe that if they were to be killed, they would go to heaven. Though Judith's religious beliefs had strayed from her father's, she still had faith on that point. But she found it difficult to be indifferent to the war, especially when she held out hope that Morgan was alive—and that his life might very well hinge on the outcome of any upcoming battles.

"Speaking of alliances," she said, "I was hoping to visit a friend of Louisa-Margaretta's today."

"You see," said Dorothy. "This is an example of how very alone I am in this era of my life. Miss Haddington has more friends in London than I do, and she has not lived here in years."

"Countess Koltsova is an old friend of her mother's," said Judith quickly.

Her stomach turned at the thought. Mrs Haddington,

blaming Judith for Louisa-Margaretta's dark state of mind some years ago, had still shown no signs of forgiveness. She seemed to believe that Judith had caused all of Louisa-Margaretta's troubles. For a time, Judith had been quite scared that Mrs Haddington would force her father out of his position as rector. Indeed, the Haddingtons had enough money to do as they liked. Fortunately, Mrs Haddington still appeared to adore Papa's sermons. She did not hold the father responsible for the sins of the child. But she had hardly been able to bring herself to look at Judith and had most likely passed on those misgivings to her friends. Countess Koltsova might not even be willing to see Judith, much less bestow favours upon her.

"Why call on her?" asked Dorothy, the bitterness in her voice fading a bit in favor of curiosity. "Do you ask for news of the Haddingtons?"

"No," said Judith hesitantly. She did not wish to tell her cousin of Morgan's silence. Dorothy would be sure that he had broken off the engagement, whereas Judith was sure there must be a different explanation. After all, her father and Aunt Leah had been very worried in their letters, and they would have tried to help Judith recover if they believed Morgan to be faithless.

Dorothy's wide green eyes still held their curious expression. "I'm host to not only you but also your friend," she said, slouching in her chair. "If you won't tell me what you're doing, I may not be so hasty about preparing your meals."

Judith looked down at the burned crumpet. Dorothy had never been an outstanding cook, and Judith knew her hired girl would be doing most of the work in the kitchen. Still, it was a fair-enough criticism. The money that Dorothy and Jasper received from their parents might be more than many could boast, but it was hardly paying for luxurious circumstances. It was as if their mother and father still believed that Jasper might be induced to choose another profession if only they could keep him living in relative penury.

"I am engaged," Judith said, feeling even more guilty as she saw that Dorothy's smile was wide and sincere. "Before you congratulate me, know that my fiancé never returned from Europe. He was at the Congress of Vienna, and he was to accompany a certain gentleman back to England."

"The Viscount Rialton," breathed Dorothy, and Judith was sorry to note that even her cousin had heard the gossip. "Oh, I see."

That man had a terrible reputation, and Judith saw that Dorothy was trying in vain to hide her horror.

"Everyone is talking of his disappearance," she said. "He has been gone for some time, ever since he left Vienna. Do you think the Koltsovs might know something?"

Judith's whole body was tight, and she made an effort to straighten her shoulders and remove the scowl from her face. Of course all of London was worried about that horrible man, when they ought to have been thinking of Morgan.

"There were two other young men with him," she said. "One of them was my intended, Mr Morgan Ramsbury."

Dorothy's face fell. "Oh, I am sorry, Judith. Only, I assumed—never mind. There has been talk of the other men, of course."

Silence fell between them, and Judith realised she had never answered her cousin's question.

"I cannot say where they are," she said. "But everyone we've consulted so far knows nothing at all. The Koltsovs, at least, know other diplomats and their families who were in Vienna. They might be able to shed some light on what happened, even if they are not certain."

"And if they truly know nothing?" asked Dorothy, meeting Judith's eyes.

Judith tried not to sigh. Her cousin could be just as difficult as Louisa-Margaretta, which was one reason she had hoped they would not be too long under the same roof. She hoped Louisa-Margaretta would continue sleeping on that particular morning, not wake up in the heat of the morning and quarrel with Dorothy.

"I'm not sure," said Judith. "But the wisest thing would be for someone to send a party along their route to look for them."

Dorothy did not bother hiding her feelings about that plan. She laughed. "When so many of our young men are off fighting Napoleon Bonaparte?"

"If necessary," said Judith. She could feel her temper rising, but she did not wish to cry in front of Dorothy. "But I hope it shall not be necessary."

"Oh, Judith," said Dorothy. "Don't be offended."

Judith hated when others told her not to be sad, offended, or worried. She felt that she had a right to these feelings, especially since she was determined not to express them in an undignified manner.

"I know what I'm asking," Judith said solemnly. "But, Dorothy, don't you understand? I have heard nothing from Morgan all this time or from anyone in his party. It does not matter that our country is at war. I am not engaged to the whole country. As I'm Mr Ramsbury's fiancée, this is the only choice that remains."

8

Louisa-Margaretta woke with a headache. The fact of the malady displeased her even more than the pain. She had long considered illness to be a sign of weak character, and she hated Mr Fortescue for making her into an invalid.

She had to wear one of her best gowns, as she knew the theatrical types placed a good deal of importance on one's attire. Attempting the right sort of hair and toilette without a maid was exceedingly difficult, and she could not get her stays fastened properly beneath the gown. She and Judith had lived in some rather challenging accommodations before, but at least there was always a friend nearby who could help with such things. Judith was gone, and Louisa-Margaretta was not about to ask Miss Dorothy St Clair for assistance. Her hostess had hardly been gracious so far.

Louisa-Margaretta only emerged once she had gotten herself into a tolerable semblance of order. In spite of the summer heat, she used a shawl to hide the lumpiness at the back of her gown, hoping that Judith would be home soon to get it into order.

"Good morning," Louisa-Margaretta said to the sour-faced Dorothy. "Where has our Miss St Clair gone off to today?"

"She is trying to get word of her Mr Ramsbury," said Dorothy. "It seems a hopeless business to me, to be perfectly honest. I'm quite sure the fellow's dead."

"Well, he is my cousin," said Louisa-Margaretta tartly. "So I'm not sure you should be speaking of him in those terms."

In spite of her objections, though, Louisa-Margaretta felt a shiver of unease. Whenever Judith expressed discontent about Morgan's whereabouts, Louisa-Margaretta always told her that dear Cousin Morgan was far too pious to ever die. Surely, he had gotten lost at some strange monastery on the journey home from Vienna. Or perhaps he was helping some lost soul. He was just as dedicated to charitable pursuits as Louisa-Margaretta's mother. Though unlike Mama, he did not take care to announce his every good intention to the world.

"I apologise," said Dorothy without sounding at all apologetic. "I put away the breakfast things. Were you hoping to eat?"

The offer was not made with any spirit, so Louisa-Margaretta shook her head, though her stomach lurched, and she realised just then that she could have eaten enough breakfast to feed an army.

"No," she said. "Thank you, but I'll wait until later."

In the silence, Louisa-Margaretta drummed her fingers on the table. "Any idea when Judith might return? Countess Koltsova rather despises independent young women, so I cannot think poor Judith will get a very warm reception."

Dorothy shook her head. "No. But I was glad to have her

here for breakfast. With Jasper keeping theatre hours, I am often alone in the morning."

Louisa-Margaretta imagined how lovely it would be to have the morning free, with no need to entertain others or tolerate her mother's lectures, but she did not say so. "Theatre hours are certainly very different from those of most young people," she said with what she hoped was a charming smile. Though she found Miss Dorothy St Clair both inhospitable and dull, her best chance of getting Mr Solier's opera performed was through the Lyceum Theatre. Since Mr Jasper St Clair appeared to have some influence with Miss Byrd, Louisa-Margaretta could hardly afford to offend his sister.

The young hostess seemed to recognise that thought, and she peered carefully at Louisa-Margaretta. "Forgive my interference," she said. "But you must know that marrying into this life is not likely to bring you happiness."

Louisa-Margaretta felt as if the words had scalded her. "Excuse me?"

"Theatre hours are terrible, and the pay is not impressive," said Miss St Clair, tossing her head as she took out her work basket. "I know that you like grand country homes, riding, hunting. There will not be a good deal of that if you are to be always in London, trying to charm people in the operatic world."

Louisa-Margaretta clenched her fists in fury. In fact, that very objection had occurred to her more than once, but she had waved it away in her mind. It seemed better to take the marriage, one that she had hastily promised after meeting Mr Solier in St Petersburg, than to keep living a dull life in Derbyshire. She also did not trust herself to be a virtuous woman. Mr Fortescue, of all people, had taught Louisa-Margaretta that her impulses and desires could be dangerous. She hoped they would be subsumed under the demands, or at least the respectability, of matrimony. And truth be told, she did think that Mr Solier was rather handsome, though she was certainly able to look at him without any undue fluttering of the heart. Perhaps passion would come with time.

"I'm sure it is easier to be a theatrical wife than a theatrical spinster," Louisa-Margaretta said flatly. "And of course I would love a grand country home, but it is not wise to suppose that I shall get one."

Her companion shrugged, poking listlessly about in her work basket without settling on any one task. "I still dream of one," she said. "You may think that is foolish."

"No more foolish than any other dream," said Louisa-Margaretta briskly. "But having lived in a grand country home, I must point out that it makes for a rather dull existence. At Wycliff Castle, if not for Judith's company, I should have died for lack of amusement."

"Oh," breathed Dorothy. "I believe I have no worries on that score. For I know myself to be happy when I have country air, a friend or two, and no financial troubles. I have spent enough time in my own family's country home to be quite certain of that."

"Then why do you not go there now?" asked Louisa-Margaretta.

Dorothy gave her a glance that was rather too knowing. "And live under my parents' control rather than have a bit of freedom here with my brother?" she asked. "I may not love London, but I cannot pretend to love the role of unmarried daughter, even if it includes a beautiful garden."

Louisa-Margaretta nodded. For once, she agreed completely with her hostess. "That is a role I shall be happy to give up myself."

"But not in this manner," said Dorothy. "Ivo Solier is a man devoted only to himself. I see enough men like that in Jasper's circles. Probably most of them, though I must say for Mr Daw that he seems devoted to his wife and very proud of the young people he has supported."

"It does not signify whether Mr Solier is an attentive husband. I can manage well enough on my own," snapped Louisa-Margaretta. "I've done so for some time."

Dorothy St Clair expertly threaded a needle and began darning one of her brother's shirts. "And that is reason enough for marriage?"

"It is reason enough," said Louisa-Margaretta, "for me to go to the theatre. I must bid you good day."

9

No amount of banging on the doors open to the public sufficed. Louisa-Margaretta was not going to be permitted to enter the theatre. Her feet were already feeling stiff and sore, as she had walked all the way from Mr St Clair's rather unfashionable neighborhood to his place of business. Louisa-Margaretta loved a long walk in the countryside, especially when it included some very fine shooting. But a long walk on the city pavements, simply because one had neither a carriage nor the funds available to hire one, was very difficult for a lady of fashion.

She knew that Mr Solier would have been given free use of a carriage where he was staying, and she felt a moment of envy. If only she had remembered her circumstances when she was speaking to Dorothy. She would have a fortune of at least thirty thousand pounds, very likely more, as her parents were so eager to see her married to the "right" sort of gentleman. But without the marriage, she was penniless and humiliated.

Well, not quite penniless, of course. She still had some

of the money she had taken with her from Derbyshire, but until the banns were read, she was not eager to squander it.

The theatre's small door for actors was also locked, but knocking got a response.

"What is it, then?" asked Miss Byrd, looking rather like a man in her dark trousers and jacket. Her face was pale. "I hope you have come prepared to work, because I had another look at the opera this morning, and I am quite convinced that all is lost."

"All is not lost," said a high, mocking voice behind her. "You will just need to choose another opera."

Louisa-Margaretta stepped into the dark passageway, blinking a bit as she left the bright sunlight for the dingy environs of the theatre's backstage areas. Though the Lyceum Theatre's candlelight was bright enough throughout the performance, there were no lovely chandeliers in the low-ceiled rooms for the actors, and since it was still early, most of them were dark.

"Good morning, my dear," said Louisa-Margaretta, giving Mr Solier a smile.

"Yes, your fiancé has been here all morning, attempting to convince me of the wisdom of my choosing one of his works for our primary performance," said Miss Byrd. "Mr Solier, if you would still like your comic opera to be performed, I would advise you to leave with all possible haste."

"I have many operas," said Mr Solier. "Any one of which would be better than Mr Mozart's silly work, with all due respect."

He said the last bit with the French mannerism of offering no respect at all, and Louisa-Margaretta almost laughed.

"The more, the better, Monsieur Solier," Miss Byrd said. "Perhaps you ought to go speak to the other theatres."

"We have been to them already. They would not know genius if it were presented to them on a platter of—"

"But," said Louisa-Margaretta, taking his arm, "you've now been offered a very lovely position at this reputable theatre. If you were to mention that you helped secure the finances here and that your opera is much anticipated, the reception at those theatres might be very different."

Louisa-Margaretta was rather satisfied with that proposition, especially the fact that she had put it to him in French. In a few short months, Ivo Solier had managed to accomplish what no governess had been able to do. He had made Louisa-Margaretta learn French, at least enough to communicate. She had always had a terrible accent and a very rudimentary grasp of grammar, but Monsieur Solier's steadfast refusal to speak English had taught her a great deal.

The Frenchman paused, thinking over the offer. "Very well," he said. "They may see things differently now that one theatre has seen the merit of my work. That is true enough. You will accompany me."

"No!" Louisa-Margaretta said and saw that Monsieur Solier was both displeased and confused.

"*Comment non*," he murmured.

"I must stay and rewrite Mr Mozart's libretto," she said. "If Mr Coleman does not take it, the finances from Mr Fortescue may fall through. Then your opera will not be introduced to London at all."

He grumbled, but he left. Miss Byrd waved him off with a smile before slamming the door closed behind him.

"You are rather late to this repair," she said. "Your friend Miss Haddington has been here for hours."

Louisa-Margaretta was not used to being scolded. "Perhaps she has the work well in hand, then."

Miss Byrd was already walking, and her steps were so quick that Louisa-Margaretta struggled to keep up. "I think not," she said. "But you can see for yourself."

She took Louisa-Margaretta to a room full of boxes. Judith was sitting at an instrument, the table next to her covered in papers.

"I'm trying to make sense of the first aria, I must confess," said Judith. "It seems Mr Coleman objected to anything that was very specific in Don Alphonso's descriptions of the ladies' behavior. But that makes the music flow rather terribly. How much are we to add, then?"

The director waved a hand at them. "We cannot have a short opera. People must stay, eat, and drink. Otherwise, even with your Mr Fortescue's money, we will have no profits at all."

"He is *not* my Mr Fortescue," said Judith.

Miss Byrd, confused, turned to the other young lady.

"He is not *my* Mr Fortescue," said Louisa-Margaretta.

The director glared at them. "Well, Mr Fortescue may stay unclaimed, but if this opera is not fixed, he will be keeping his money."

"It will be," said Louisa-Margaretta firmly. "But Londoners will not like these silly names at all. Miss St Clair, we must rechristen them at once. Perhaps the ladies can be Deborah and Flora, with the maid's name being Sarah. That is Mrs Daw's Christian name, is it not?"

"Yes," said Miss Byrd just as Judith said "No!" and shrank in horror.

The director peered at Judith. "I think different names would be much better," she said. "I shall leave the two of you to it, then."

"Thank you," said Judith, her smile turning cold as the director's brisk footsteps faded away.

10

____

"We must get all this done, I suppose." Louisa-Margaretta sighed. "There is to be another rehearsal tonight. The actors will have to memorise everything we change. So we can't write too much that is new. They will never learn it."

"Pardon," said Judith. "Do you have any interest in my morning?"

"No," said Louisa-Margaretta, "not particularly. Why? Did you see anything interesting on your walk here?"

Judith stared at her. "I was brought here in a carriage," she said. "I came from the Koltsovs'."

"Oh, a carriage," said Louisa-Margaretta. "How marvelous that must be! I cannot think how your dear cousin gets from this place to his quarters every day, especially when he's tired. It is not a pleasant walk at all."

Judith looked down at the keys of the instrument then back at her friend. "Louisa-Margaretta," she said. "Why are we speaking of my cousin when we ought to be speaking of yours? Morgan is still missing, and Countess Koltsova could promise nothing!"

"I don't see what good talking does," said Louisa-Margaretta. "If the Koltsovs knew where he was, I'm sure they would have him brought back."

Judith stood, the bench rattling as she walked over to Louisa-Margaretta. "Somebody must bring him back," she said. "And if the influence of the Koltsovs and all your other rich friends does nothing, I shall go myself."

Louisa-Margaretta let out a sharp laugh. "Why, Judith, that is madness!"

"Much madness is divinest sense," said Miss Byrd, who had come back to the room. "How are you getting on? I have to tell the actors not to come tonight if we have nothing for them, you know."

Judith swallowed, edging closer to the pianoforte. It would be a terrible disappointment to Jasper if the performances were cancelled. He and Dorothy had both been quite open about how difficult it had been for him to find work. Miss Byrd was not the only one who felt that the war with France would mean a very dismal time for those in the theatrical business.

"We're getting along rather well," said Judith. "Louisa-Margaretta had some ideas for the names. That is, the gentlemen as well."

Without needing to be told, Louisa-Margaretta sat down at the little table and ticked off the names. "Don Alphonso is easy enough for any Londoner, I should say. We shall change Guglielmo to George, and Ferrando can be Frederick. That makes them seem like simple country boys, which they are, at least in spirit."

Miss Byrd looked placated if not pleased. "What did you do about this part of the exchange between Despina and the ladies?" she asked them, indicating part of a page that was in front of Judith. "Or Sarah and the ladies. I'm sorry. It will seem too abrupt for their conversation to end in such a manner."

"No," said Judith. "It is rather perfect. We can end the line of music just so, and the entrance of the two gentlemen will provide the reason for them to finish their conversation."

"Only music," said the director, troubled. "Should they not say something?"

"Of course," said Louisa-Margaretta. And she sang in her practised and expressive voice, "We must leave off your ramblings, silly though you think us. Our two beaus are ambling up the walk to greet us!"

The director raised her eyebrows. "It would work well enough," she said.

"Yes," said Louisa-Margaretta. "And there are many other places where we can leave the music, only make the translation rather vaguer."

"More delicate," amended Judith. "To avoid offending the censor or any members of the audience."

Louisa-Margaretta smiled again. "Miss St Clair and I can manage quite well," she said, going over to rest a hand on Judith's shoulder.

Judith smiled up at her friend then played a chord or two. "We're well on our way," she said.

Theirs was such a friendship that the memory of easier times was enough to enable them to lie convincingly. They could pretend to get along well because they had often done so.

And even when Miss Byrd left, they got on rather well with their task, though Judith did not speak to Louisa-Margaretta again of the plans for Morgan. In fact, she had not realised her own intention until she spoke it aloud. But of course she could go to Europe then try to go along the route that Morgan had taken. Her father and sister might not wish it, but it had been some years since they had been able to stop Judith from taking such steps. And she had the evidence of her good sense behind her. After all, she had been firmly decided in favor of going to St Petersburg with Louisa-Margaretta and their friends. And they had returned home from Russia with a suitable fiancé for Louisa-Margaretta, something that had once seemed an impossibility. Judith felt that Mrs Haddington, who had been trying to marry Louisa-Margaretta off for years, ought to be very pleased with her now. Perhaps she would decide that dear Miss St Clair was not such a terrible influence on her only daughter.

Louisa-Margaretta seemed happy enough to compose with Judith, hardly stopping until Mr Solier returned. When he entered the room, her demeanor changed.

"How did you fare at the other establishments?" she asked briskly.

He only shook his head. "London is a terrible city for my profession," he said darkly. "I never thought I would miss my exile in cold, lonely Russia!"

"Not to worry," said Louisa-Margaretta. "Your star will rise here too. Only I'm afraid we need to introduce you to rather more people. Perhaps your hosts know of a ball or some hostess who is looking to make up the numbers at her table."

Mr Solier walked quickly over to the papers on the table, picked one up, then just as quickly put it down again. "What do I care for such frivolous places? I had enough balls in St Petersburg to last me the rest of my life. I need to be writing more operas, to see what life the performers breathe into my work!"

Louisa-Margaretta frowned. Judith realised that her

exact expression, the features that looked cross along with the eyes that carefully watched Mr Solier's outburst, was becoming an oft-used one. Louisa-Margaretta used to be quite often happy, but that was no longer the case. Since the engagement had begun, there had been a brief period of relief. But it had been followed by Louisa-Margaretta's strong, stubborn personality changing by the day. It was as if she were trying to beat her spirit into a wifelier shape but never quite succeeding.

"Let us go out and get something to eat," said Louisa-Margaretta. "Denounce society all you like, but one cannot underestimate the importance of a very good dinner."

11

———————

"Why, what a divine blessing," said a familiar voice. "We were so set on having a perfect dinner that we arrived early. And who should we find but Miss Haddington in London once again!"

After a rather lackluster meal at an establishment near the theatre, Louisa-Margaretta, Judith, and Mr Solier had returned to their work. As they entered the little music room, Louisa-Margaretta was surprised by a voice that she had once known very well. It took her a moment to place it. She had gotten far enough away from her childhood environs that she could hardly recall that time, and when she did, it was with a strange mixture of delight and regret.

She turned round to see one of her childhood friends, Mr Anthony Beecham, walking in with a companion she half recognised. Both of them were in the blue-and-buff uniform of the Beefsteak Club. Louisa-Margaretta knew that the members did not wish to refer to it as a club, but she could scarcely think of what else to call an organization that demanded such conformity of its members.

"Mr Beecham," she said, though she had to stop herself from calling him Anthony. He had once been a very beloved companion of her brother Percival, and Louisa-Margaretta had loved running about his family's estate with her favourite brother. Since then, she had heard a great deal about Mr Beecham, but since his ascent in the ranks of Parliament, she had rarely met with him.

He had never been the most handsome of men but had the advantage of both health and relative youth. Louisa-Margaretta thought he must be about thirty-three years old and found it rather odd that he had never married. She remembered asking Percival about it, but her brother had not been interested.

"A politician like that ought to be married to his work," Percival had grunted at the time. "Not very fair to a family, is it, then? He would have no time for them at all."

It had been a rather strange comment coming from Percival, who had once neglected his wife most dreadfully, but it made sense.

Louisa-Margaretta smoothed her hands on her skirts. She wished to put off the moment when she would be forced to tell the impressive old companion that she was engaged to an ill-tempered Frenchman, but politeness would not allow her to delay the introductions.

"This is my dear friend Miss Judith St Clair, and my fiancé, Monsieur Ivo Solier, lately of France."

Mr Beecham gave a very pleasing bow to both. "Miss St Clair, it is an honour. And Monsieur Solier, welcome to London! May I introduce you both to my own friend Mr Jonah Cartwright?"

His companion stepped forward. Mr Cartwright was a stout young man, very well dressed, and plainly eager to make a good impression.

"How did you all come to be here?" asked Mr Beecham. "I know how well you've always gotten on with the lads, dear Miss Haddington, but I'm afraid that our club is restricted to men."

"It must be a terrible club, then," said Louisa-Margaretta, not bothering to smile.

Mr Beecham and his friend laughed at her comment.

"It is," said Mr Cartwright. "Don't know why Beecham convinced me to join it. Some of the members are too old to remember what week it is. Others cheat at cards—"

"Now, then," said Mr Beecham, patting his friend's back heartily. "I'm sure it isn't so bad, or you wouldn't have come this time."

"I'm not sure we should be eating beefsteak when there is a war on," grumbled Mr Cartwright. "If we are to do something frivolous, perhaps a trip to the country. Fresh air, the races, the beauty—"

"We're to meet with this group, and that is final," said Mr Beecham firmly. "But Miss Haddington and Miss St Clair, we must dine together while you are in London. And Mr Solier, I should love to introduce you to more of my friends here in London."

"Of course," said Louisa-Margaretta warmly, though she noticed that neither Judith nor Mr Solier made any reply.

Before she could respond, she saw the other members of the club filing past the room, some with whom she could claim an acquaintance, stopping to touch their hats.

One of them was Mr Fortescue.

12

J udith shrank from Mr Fortescue. It troubled her to see that Louisa-Margaretta was also shrinking, moving close into the room as if she might disappear into the instrument.

"I am leaving," Mr Solier said with a sniff. "Nobody has invited me to this little club, though I am not a woman."

"It's meant to be very exclusive," said Judith. "They only have a score of members, and I daresay many of the men in London would love an invitation."

"They have no regard for art or for those of us who were forced out of France when they let that tyrant run rampant," said Mr Solier. "Well, then. It is a loss for their group, but I shall eat better things than their beefsteak."

He left with no warmer farewell than that, and Judith sat down next to the pianoforte again.

"I suppose we could get some of the beefsteak if we asked," said Louisa-Margaretta. "At least that explains the smell! What a strange custom, to cook food in a theatre."

"I'm sure that Miss Byrd needs every shilling they can

get," said Judith thoughtfully. "And for such men, I imagine the setting provides some sort of novelty."

Louisa-Margaretta shook her head, shoving a sheaf of papers aside so she could lean on the table.

"Honestly, Mr Solier was quite right about all this snobbery. The menu, the ridiculous uniforms... It is just an excuse for conceited revelry. I'm sure they could not be speaking of anything important! They just want to drink wine with other silly men."

"There is a war," said Judith, her stomach in knots once again. "I daresay they are speaking of that. Most of us are."

Louisa-Margaretta's laughter was so loud that Judith worried the beefsteak group would hear her. "Yes, they will talk of Napoleon Bonaparte, just like every wretch on a street corner! One needs no special invitation to indulge in that topic of conversation."

Judith held a handkerchief in the pocket of her dress, worrying the worn fabric. "Do you suppose Mr Fortescue is a regular member of their club, then?"

When Louisa-Margaretta made no answer, all the compassion that had deserted Judith earlier returned. She went to her friend, putting a hand on her shoulder.

"Oh, Louisa-Margaretta! You can't allow him to make you miserable again. Not when you have gone so far to get free of him."

"Thank you, Judith," said Louisa-Margaretta, straightening up. She was too tall for Judith to embrace her easily. "I do not ask him to threaten me, and I certainly do not seek him out."

Judith rubbed her eyes. "I know, but there must be some way to get free of him!"

"Not an easy way," said Louisa-Margaretta. "Even after I

marry Mr Solier, I suppose he shall take delight in tormenting me."

"Very well," said Judith. "But might it help to know what he's discussing now?"

Louisa-Margaretta stared at her. "What did you have in mind?"

13

The members of the club dined strictly at four p.m. Judith, though she was still hungry after the sorry portions they had eaten, insisted that they not interfere with any of the arrangements by trying to obtain any of the food requisitioned for the club. Louisa-Margaretta, who constantly complained of starvation, bribed the cook.

The two ladies ate their beefsteak in one of the highest boxes, putting the dishes on their laps and mopping up as much of the liquid as they could with bread to avoid spills.

"I cannot believe I didn't think of this," murmured Louisa-Margaretta. "A box is the perfect place to hide."

For a performance, the entire theatre would be as bright as day, with enough candles to allow the fashionable attendees to observe both the actors and one another. But for the purposes of the club, only the candles on the stage had been lit, casting the rest of the space into darkness.

Judith gave a modest smile. "The whole space is designed to allow one to easily observe what is passing on the stage," she said. "And if these gentlemen are eating and drinking onstage, they would be simpletons indeed to believe themselves always unobserved."

Louisa-Margaretta laughed, and Judith hastened to remind her that the men were not quite stupid enough to misidentify a woman's laughter.

But their own group was loudly conversing. They had opened the wine already, but it seemed that one or two conversations still continued to dominate the table.

"An opera," said one of the young gentlemen, whom Judith had heard referred to as Hartsock. "Ah, how I wish I could give up my estate to stay in London and write an opera!"

"If you wish to write an opera, then write one," said John Giles, whom Judith recognised as one of London's most popular composers of English-language plays and operas. She felt a pang for Mr Solier. Though she did not appreciate his disregard for Louisa-Margaretta or his continual rudeness, she knew that he really ought to be invited to the group. They had a great many members who were involved in the arts. And though she would never say it quite so plainly, Mr Solier's arrogance was made slightly more tolerable by its accuracy. Judith thought his music was every bit as good as what Wolfgang Amadeus Mozart had written though significantly different in terms of style, and she was surprised that the English theatrical gentlemen were not yet able to appreciate it.

"You should write an opera," said Mr Fortescue with a cunning smile. "Mrs Hartsock can go to the devil!"

A great deal of laughter all around followed. Louisa-Margaretta glared at the men. "You can go to the devil, Fortescue," she said under her breath.

"We must not say such things," said Judith without thinking. Her upbringing would not allow her to let any curses go by. Indeed, even if she had been at the table with the men and all their wine, she would have at least shaken her head. Though shy, she could not sit absolutely quiet in the face of such blasphemy.

"I know poor Mrs Hartsock," said Louisa-Margaretta. "She is only Susannah Kemp, a friend from my childhood."

"Does she disapprove of opera, then?" asked Judith with some sympathy. Her own father had always been rather liberal in his view of theatres and entertainment. Though he continued to disapprove of Jasper's choice of acting as a profession, he thought that attending plays was something that a God-fearing family could do in moderation. And because of the St Clair family's pecuniary situation, they were never able to afford such entertainment more than a few times in a year. But Judith was well aware that there were stricter clergymen, those who thought that even reading a novel should never be allowed.

"I'm sure she does not disapprove," said Louisa-Margaretta through clenched teeth. "She might simply prefer that her husband occasionally think of his duties to the home and family rather than gadding about with men like Mr Beecham and Mr Cartwright."

"I thought Mr Beecham was a great friend of yours," said Judith, alarmed by the way Louisa-Margaretta's face had flushed with anger.

She shook her head. "Of course he was. And Mr Beecham, being a bachelor, is perhaps not exactly letting the side down in his more worthy pursuits. I believe he works a great deal. But when he is not working, he is drinking, gambling, and probably doing plenty of other things with Mr Cartwright, Mr Hartsock, and others like them."

"It seems to be the case with many men of their means," said Judith. She did not say that the number included

Louisa-Margaretta's own brothers, but her friend gave her a pointed look.

"Many men of my sort—is that what you're implying? Yes, it is. But the men, not the women. The men do as they like, and for all their money, the women cannot expect the same freedom."

Judith did not respond. The talk of the men at the table had turned to war. They were speaking of what they would do to the French were they to arrive in London, hearts intent on conquering English soil. Judith did not even bother listening to that talk. Many men had already left to fight, and the men who had stayed behind would be busy inventing episodes of bravado for themselves.

"If the French were to come here," she mused, "I suppose we would have to go back to Derbyshire."

Louisa-Margaretta sighed. "No, Judith!" she said. "I am supposed to marry Mr Solier to avoid Wycliff Castle. If I never see it again, I shall not mourn. I want to travel like the Chatel ladies. Perhaps not to Russia but to Rome this time."

Judith tried not to show her hurt. "And what of me?" she asked bravely. "Am I to return to Derbyshire alone?"

She did not say that she would never return to Derbyshire if she could not find Morgan. That possibility, in the moment, seemed particularly unpleasant.

Louisa-Margaretta shook her head. "Come with us! Your family can spare you, especially now Miriam is grown."

"Yes, but how are we to travel during a war?" asked Judith. She watched her friend with care, wondering if Louisa-Margaretta was marrying only for the opportunity to leave England again. Though Madame Chatel seemed rather stoic on the subject of travel, not complaining even when she was indisposed for weeks on the voyage from England to Russia, Judith knew that she would have preferred to continue to live in Paris rather than eking out a living in exile. And Mademoiselle Chatel dreamed of nothing more than a simple cottage where she could cook and entertain friends, though her mother derided that vision as both common and improper. If the Chatels were Louisa-Margaretta's ideal, she had chosen poorly.

Louisa-Margaretta gestured to the men on the stage. "Listen to what they're saying," she said. "This little war will all be over soon," she said. "The upstart Napoleon Bonaparte cannot bring Europe to its knees again. He does not have the army he had, and some of the French are already rebelling against him."

"I cannot pretend to know," said Judith. "Only I recall the last time very well. We were told that the fighting would be short."

Louisa-Margaretta gazed down at the stage. "Well, I ought not to make any plans for traveling anyway. Mr Fortescue is determined to see me break my engagement."

Judith squinted down at the men. The stage was so well lit that she was fairly certain they would not have seen her, even if she had sat openly in the box rather than huddling on its floor with Louisa-Margaretta and peering over the railing.

"If only Mr Fortescue would travel," she mused.

Louisa-Margaretta gave a choked laugh. Some of Mr Fortescue's ancestors had been from China, but that seemed to interest him only insofar as his expensive collection of pottery.

"He has no interest in going to the Orient, more's the pity," Louisa-Margaretta said. "Such a journey would take him away for years."

"And he does not wish to join the fighting in France, I'm

sure," said Judith. "A man who insists on his own way at all times would make a poor soldier."

Louisa-Margaretta took her fork and stabbed at some of the beefsteak that Judith had left uneaten. Judith, who had been planning to eat all of the food before her, did not complain.

"Mr Fortescue ought to die," said Louisa-Margaretta between mouthfuls of beefsteak. "That is the only way we shall ever be rid of him."

Judith gasped, staring at her friend.

"I know you don't wish me to say it," continued Louisa-Margaretta. "But he loves power too much to stop being a blackmailer. And I should be thankful that he has only tried to threaten me into marriage! Young women who hold his interest might face much worse."

Judith's heart sank. She knew Mr Fortescue had a history of wooing women then abandoning them when the initial attraction ceased or when the inconvenience of a child presented itself. And given the opportunity, he might have tried to do the same with Louisa-Margaretta. She was thankful that her friend had seen Mr Fortescue for what he was before his attempts at seduction succeeded. But she knew Louisa-Margaretta was still deeply ashamed of her original feelings for Mr Fortescue. It was one thing to bestow one's affection on an unworthy recipient but another thing entirely to be entrapped by such a villain.

"He must have a weakness," said Judith. "I never thought he would make good on his threats if you simply failed to marry him. But if you do marry another, he shall have no very good reason to stay in your good graces."

"Exactly," said Louisa-Margaretta. "Do you think we could trick him into fighting a duel with one of those young men then sabotage his pistol?"

Judith groaned. "Please," she said. "There must be another solution."

"I could shoot him myself," mused Louisa-Margaretta. "As you are aware, I am an excellent shot."

Judith did not dignify that with a response. Instead, she watched as the group on the stage grew more raucous. They had paid the cook, and they began to break into their own little groups. The air was soon thick with the smell of cigar smoke. Even from a great distance, Judith was bothered by it. She began to feel ill.

"There is not an easy way to get rid of Mr Fortescue," said Louisa-Margaretta briskly. "But one problem at a time. We must finish our work before the actors arrive. For tonight, Mr Solier and I are still engaged, and it would not do to displease him."

He will be displeased no matter what we do, thought Judith. *He is simply the sort of man who is never pleased.*

But she was wise enough not to say it out loud.

14

———

The Beefsteak men often stayed out until the small hours of the morning. However, when the club's prohibitions against nonmembers, women, and most forms of entertainment began to grate on the younger members, the group always adjourned to some other haunt for the night. That generally began to happen around eight o'clock in the evening.

The actors were just beginning to arrive, along with Mr Solier, as the members left the stage. The women who had been cooking were efficient cleaners, and Judith looked at the stage with some trepidation. Soon, the music she had spent the day writing would be performed. *What a strange thrill!* If she were not so worried about its reception, she would feel only joy. For the first time, she understood more of Mr Solier's mindset. Of course he was determined to go about London, begging everyone to perform his operas. If one were confident, as he was, it must be the most gratifying thing in the world.

Miss Sweet was standing in one of the wings off the

stage, conferring with Mrs Daw, when Mr Fortescue came over.

"Ladies!" he said. "I cannot wait to hear this little opera I'm purchasing. I have heard that even your names are different. Though a Miss Sweet by any other name would look just as *sweet*, I assure you."

"I have not yet seen the revisions, sir," said Miss Sweet. "But your patronage is much appreciated."

Though the young woman's face was all sincerity, Judith did not fail to note the phrasing. She said that Mr Fortescue's patronage was "appreciated" but failed to say by whom. It was an elegant way of veiling an insult.

"And after the rehearsal," he said carefully, "would you and your fellow actresses deign to take a meal with me, or are you honoring the Duke of Ormonde with your presence?"

Judith tried in vain to hide her horror. Of course, she had heard rumours about Miss Sweet and the duke from more than one source and even seen the young actress leaving with her older patron. But for all that, Judith would never have mentioned it. She had encountered more than one woman who earned her living through dubious means, because of both her father's status as a clergyman and her mother's particular kindness to the women. In fact, Mama had always been so adamant about ladies who made their living on the stage being underpaid and ill-treated that Judith felt instinctive sympathy for Miss Sweet. And that was accompanied by guilt. She had written her father only a few short lines, saying that she had returned to London and was staying with her cousins, neglecting to mention that she was involved in the theatre. He would not approve. It was one thing to go and see an opera but another thing entirely to be moving about backstage, waiting for the last men of the Beefsteak Club to leave so she might support the production.

Mr Beecham approached the little group with two of his friends just as Mr Fortescue raised his eyebrows, plainly expecting a response.

Miss Sweet gave a cool smile. "I have not decided," she said. "I imagine this rehearsal may be rather taxing."

"Taxing, eh?" asked Mr Beecham, who was laughing with his friends Mr Hartsock and Mr Cartwright. "Well, I wish you all the best, Miss Sweet. We could use a good production. The last time I managed to see a play, it was terribly dull."

"Because it was not an opera, and it had no Miss Sweet," said Mr Fortescue.

Mr Beecham was too much of a politician to insult the man outright, but Judith noticed that his smile dimmed a bit when he answered.

"Miss Sweet is indeed an excellent singer," he said with a bow to the young lady. "Mr Fortescue, are you joining us?"

Mr Beecham's companions looked at each other, but Mr Fortescue only laughed.

"Unfortunately, I am needed here!" he said. "But do leave some cigars and wine for me in case this production is not as interesting as I had hoped."

"I'm sure you may go with your friends if you'd like," said Judith rather too quickly. Though she despised Mr Fortescue, she found it very hard to speak against him. It was rather like being near a mad dog—one had to be very certain of one's defenses.

Mr Fortescue only smiled. "I would like to see what sort of production I'm buying here, thank you, my dear Miss St Clair," he said, his gallantry tinged with mockery. "But I will have my cigars if little Mr Cartwright here will fetch them. Perhaps you would like to sit with me?"

"She is needed in the ladies' dressing room," said Miss Sweet swiftly. "There is nobody to help us today."

As she showed Judith to the dressing room, Miss Sweet took her leave of the other gentlemen.

"Enjoy your evening!" she said.

Not until they were in the dressing room did she speak again.

"You needn't stay long," Miss Sweet said, locking the door behind her.

Mrs Daw was looking carefully in a mirror, adding precise lines to her face. Miss Wynn, who was wearing an ordinary dress with a large shawl, was absorbed in a book.

"Don't you need help with dressing?" asked Judith.

Miss Sweet shook her head. "No, we can manage. We aren't going to be wearing most of the costumes anyway, only when Miss Byrd specifically requests it. But Mr Fortescue is not the sort of man to leave us alone. In fact, like many patrons, I'm sure he would be in this room with us now if it were not locked."

Judith's face must have shown her apprehension, for Mrs Daw shook her head. Without taking her eyes off her reflection in the mirror, she addressed Judith.

"That sort of thing doesn't happen in this theatre," she said. "It's because of Miss Byrd. Not to worry, dear. He can pay for as many operas as he likes. He won't be welcome in here."

She said it as if it were reassuring. Judith took it as only another example of the corrupt nature of the whole place and felt ill.

"I wonder if we ought to find another patron," she said.

Miss Wynn looked up from her reading. "He's one of the

worst ones," she said. "But he is good for the money. See to it that you don't end up alone with him. You'll be just fine. Stay with that sister of yours."

Judith gave a sad smile. "My only sister is in Derbyshire. I haven't seen her for almost a year." And she felt homesick once more, eager to learn more of Miriam and her brothers than their few letters could tell her. How she wished she could go home, if only for a brief visit. But with nobody else eager to look for Morgan, she could not seek the comforts of her family's hearth quite yet.

A loud gong sounded, and Miss Wynn sighed. "Well, I hope the opera you're presenting us with is a decent one, Miss St Clair," she said. "I would rather learn dozens of new lines than have it all be for nothing."

Judith hastened to reassure her. "We made as few changes as possible, really! I hope it shall not be too hard to learn."

Mrs Daw unlocked the door, scanning the ladies to make sure they were all perfectly ready. "We shall learn them," she said, leading the way into the green room. "We always do."

"Miss Sweet excepted," said Miss Wynn.

Judith looked away. She had wondered how long it would take for the animosity to resurface between the two.

"I do not need to learn the lines," said Miss Sweet. "I could sing nothing but tra-la-la, and all London would admire my voice. Especially in comparison to yours."

"Are the two of you f-fighting again?" asked Mr Nightingale. His voice marked him as a man who stuttered regularly, not from any particular trouble or nervous temperament. He did not seem at all distressed, only amused.

"Always," said Miss Sweet and Miss Wynn in unison.

Judith almost laughed, but she didn't wish for them to be angry with her.

"Judith," said Jasper, who was hastening to rejoin the group. "Come. Miss Byrd has been asking for you. You and Miss Haddington are to stay with her. With any luck, she will be happy with some of what you've done, but I have no doubt she will ask for many more changes."

On seeing her expression, he burst out laughing. "It's the nature of the theatre, Judith! Many changes are required. *C'est la vie.*"

"*Oui,*" murmured Judith. Unlike Louisa-Margaretta, she had always spoken French well, and the time she'd spent with Mr Solier had only helped her perfect her accent. "*C'est la vie.*"

As she watched Jasper and Mr Nightingale take their positions onstage for the first scene alongside Mr Daw, a different French phrase came to mind: *bête de scène.* Mr Nightingale's stammer vanished, as did Jasper's weariness and Mr Daw's boasting. All three of them were so well suited to their parts that Judith found herself lost in the story, though the men were relying on the pages she and Louisa-Margaretta had hastily copied out with all the revisions. Even squinting at the parchment half the time, they embodied their roles so well that Judith was sure the show would be a success.

15

———

"This opera will be a dismal failure!" shouted Miss Byrd, stopping the rehearsal. "What is this nonsense about the two young men going away to help a sick relation in the countryside?"

Louisa-Margaretta stood straighter, walking onto the stage next to the director. "It was a necessary change," she said, her voice nearly as loud, though she thought shouting would be beneath her. "Mr Coleman would not allow such a funny opera about soldiers. We are not to mock anyone who wears such a uniform."

The director covered her face. "What urgency is there here?" she moaned. "These two young men are supposed to be lovesick! They would not leave for such a minor obligation."

"It was the easiest thing to put in, given the constraints of the music," said Judith quietly without venturing onto the stage.

"I can't hear you, Miss St Clair!" said Miss Byrd. "Think of the people at the back of the theatre."

It must have been an instruction she employed habitually, for Louisa-Margaretta knew well that the back of the theatre was empty. The whole theatre, in fact, was empty except for the place where Mr Fortescue had been sitting. But he was coming backstage, speaking in a low voice with the ladies who were due to go onstage.

"Perhaps they could be going to a funeral instead," said Judith, some desperation in her voice. "It was for a dear friend of theirs, so they're conflicted, but there is an obligation."

"Dear Miss St Clair, do you not think they would be rogues and give it up?" asked Mr Daw. "They would convince themselves that their obligation was to the living."

Miss Byrd frowned but looked as if she might allow herself to be convinced. She crossed her arms, listening to the actors discuss the matter with Judith, who was blushing madly.

Mr Fortescue's arm was around Miss Sweet's shoulders. He was leaning in to murmur to her. Louisa-Margaretta began walking over, concerned by the look of paralyzed hatred on Miss Sweet's pale features.

But Miss Wynn made her way to the couple first, pushing Miss Sweet aside.

"You cosy up to every patron we've ever had," she said loudly, sticking out her chin. "I must speak plainly, Miss Sweet. This absolutely disgusts me."

She turned a charming smile to Mr Fortescue. "You, sir, ought to be careful. I am prettier than Miss Sweet, but I expect a great deal more from my admirers."

Mrs Daw clucked at both of them. "Mr Daw is calling us," she said, taking the two ladies' arms and leading them over to the little conference in the middle of the stage.

Louisa-Margaretta went to stand next to Mr Fortescue,

hoping he would not take the same liberties he had with Miss Sweet. Usually, he pretended to respect her when others were watching. Perhaps with actresses, he did not have the same compunctions.

She noticed that Mr Nightingale was talking animatedly to Mr Daw. In spite of the noticeable stutter, his speaking voice was almost as melodious as his singing voice. But Louisa-Margaretta had no time to dwell on what the actors were saying. Mr Fortescue was speaking to her, keeping his voice just low enough that others wouldn't hear.

"Ah, my future wife," he said, grinning again. "I am sure that you have had some time to think over my offer. If a year was insufficient, now you have had over a year! What a generous man I am."

"I have thought of your offer," said Louisa-Margaretta. "And I've decided to sue you for blackmail."

"Ah yes, the legal remedy," said Mr Fortescue. "I have heard a great deal about this, of course. Yet as I told you, I have never seen it come to pass."

Louisa-Margaretta stared at the actors, keeping her gaze fixed on their expressions. Mrs Daw's skirts swished about as she demonstrated some stage directions, and the loud guffaw that Mr Nightingale gave was almost enough to cheer her.

"Well, it shall come to pass," said Louisa-Margaretta. "Or you can abandon this charade. There are plenty of women in London who would be willing to marry you."

"Yes," said Mr Fortescue. "But there is only one intelligent, desirable woman who has had the courage to refuse me directly. Though certainly, several ladies made me understand that their affections were otherwise engaged, even when I could see through the lies."

Louisa-Margaretta didn't answer. She had known for

some time that her temper and her frankness, more than anything, were what had drawn Mr Fortescue to her. At one time, she had even considered marriage with him, at least before she fully understood his character.

"My family has powerful connections," she said. "And I intend to bury you."

"Your family's power stems almost entirely from money," said Mr Fortescue. "And as one who can say much the same, I am all for that sort of power. But I ask you, what of your father's business interests? If they are to evaporate, how shall you bring the full force of the law against me?"

"Mr Fudge is not so easily corruptible," said Louisa-Margaretta. And though she was fairly certain of the magistrate, she could not pretend to be indifferent to Mr Fortescue's threats. "You could not harm my father's interests."

Mr Fortescue beamed. "Oh, but indeed, I could! Then not only the Haddingtons' reputation but also their very worth would be all but gone. What a tragedy!"

Louisa-Margaretta glared at him. "If we were married, I'm sure you would make such threats on a daily basis."

He blinked innocently. "Threats? I have never made a threat in my life. But if some have chosen to misinterpret my words, well, I can hardly control others."

"Lies don't suit you," snapped Louisa-Margaretta.

"Well, poverty would not suit you, my flower," said Mr Fortescue. "So perhaps you should consider your actions more closely."

When she did not respond, he smiled again. "My dear cook sent a great deal of food with me," he said. "I intend to sit just below the stage and watch this little spectacle. Would you care to join me?"

Louisa-Margaretta, who was in fact still rather hungry, stormed back onto the stage just as the actors were leaving.

The women were getting into their places, and the men were standing in the wings, ready to make a triumphant entrance.

"Come," said Judith. "We have settled on the funeral, but we have a great deal of work still before us."

16

Judith wrote frantically while Louisa-Margaretta paced. The detail of the funeral was a small one, but it affected many of the lines that were to come. She had snatched the actors' copies from them in a hurry then gone to work amending them as best she could. The two suitors, she had decided, could remain gentlemen of leisure. It would be best to choose that same category for the false personas the men adopted. Instead of soldiers pretending to be other soldiers, as in Mr Mozart's version, they would be dilettantes pretending to be other dilettantes. Because of the societal position of the men, it really would have been more appropriate for them to be clergymen or some other type of military men. But any profession might make them fall afoul of Mr Coleman's sensibilities, so she didn't dare risk such a thing.

"Louisa-Margaretta," said Judith, attempting to make her tone stern. "I've still got the third act left, if you feel inclined to make any alterations."

Louisa-Margaretta, as was her wont, chose to ignore the implied rebuke.

"I don't feel like making any alterations at all," she said. "How can I, when I must solve this problem of Mr Fortescue?"

Mr Solier chose that moment to enter. "I am not sure this sorry little opera is worth all the trouble," he said.

Judith blinked. "I'm sure it will be."

"Yes, if only because it allows you to have your London debut, dear, and not a moment too soon," said Louisa-Margaretta in English.

Judith wondered if that was how her friend's life was to be in the future. When she was cross, which would be often, she would mutter things in English so her husband would not understand. She had heard enough stories about marriage to know that was the way with many couples, but she hoped it was not true for Louisa-Margaretta.

"I hope your silly censor accepts my opera," said Mr Solier. "It is in better taste than this one, certainly. But still—"

"I also hope he accepts it," said Louisa-Margaretta. "But if he does not, you may be certain that Judith and I shall do the revisions. We are getting rather good at them. Now, go find a seat in one of the boxes and wait for us."

When he left, Judith was on the verge of saying that *she* was becoming skilled at revisions, whereas much of the time, Louisa-Margaretta simply inhabited the same rooms as the piles of parchment. But Louisa-Margaretta seized the third act and began going through the papers with alacrity.

"Would you like to talk about him?" said Judith.

"No," said Louisa-Margaretta shortly.

"You didn't ask whether I meant Mr Fortescue or Mr Solier," said Judith.

"It does not signify," said Louisa-Margaretta. "We shall

speak of no men except for the three gentlemen who appear in this opera."

17

___

Judith and Louisa-Margaretta got on so well that they didn't see the stage again until the third act, as they spent all of the second revising the latter part of the opera. By the time they emerged, the actors were in the middle of a sanitized version of the final scene.

"Mr and Mrs Daw, Mr St Clair, Miss Wynn," said Miss Byrd. Her voice was still clear after so many hours. "You are all much too close. This is supposed to be an opera for Mr Coleman's sensibilities, so act as if you're strangers."

She sighed. "Softer, Mr Nightingale. Your voice is supposed to be in harmony with the others'."

Amid the stream of directions, the singers managed to get through the final notes, and Judith was relieved to see that their smiles were not wholly false. As they finished, Jasper looked over to the side of the stage and winked at her.

"Bravo, bravo!" came Mr Fortescue's voice. He had a slight cough.

Judith was sure that smoking as many cigars as he had could not be good for one's health. Her father had always held that sweets, alcohol, and tobacco ought to be largely avoided, and Mr Fortescue might be proving that point.

She wondered, in fact, if alcohol was not just as much to blame as the cigars. A great deal of the port that was left over from the Beefsteak Club had made its way into Mr Fortescue's hands, and Judith had seen him taking long swigs from a glass throughout the rehearsal.

"We should do the curtain call," said Mr Daw.

"I'm not b-bowing for that idiot," said Mr Nightingale.

Miss Byrd shook her head. "He's paying," she said firmly. "And it makes no difference. You will bow when all sorts of scoundrels are in the audience. Why not this scoundrel?"

Jasper shot a nervous look at the ladies. "We shouldn't subject them to such a man," he said.

Mr Daw sighed. "Youth! They will be subjected to many such men, and this one has deep pockets. Be thankful he has nothing rotten to throw. Miss St Clair, Miss Haddington, perhaps you would go around to one of the sides, and we shall practise our motions. The curtain is too heavy, but we ought never to miss an opportunity to practise."

Jasper looked as if he were ready to protest again, but Miss Wynn touched his arm.

Judith and Louisa-Margaretta left the stage by some stairs around the side, taking care to stay well away from Mr Fortescue. He was slumping in his seat, indolent in the grip of the port and the late hour, and Judith was thankful that they could turn their attention to the stage.

The director began singing the music the orchestra was to play. Her voice was not nearly as loud as any of the actors', but it was pleasing nonetheless. Her sense of pitch was excellent.

Judith and Louisa-Margaretta applauded heavily. Only when all the actors stood together, joining hands and beaming at their imagined audience, did Judith notice Mr Fortescue.

She looked over at him just as he fell out of his chair.

"Help!" she cried. "Mr Fortescue is unwell."

The actors looked at one another.

Mrs Daw was the first to make her way down the stairs, though she did not hurry. "He is drunk, more like," she said quietly. "Go along, then, girls. We shan't let him sleep here all night, but there's no need to disturb him just now."

Mr Daw had followed closely, and he got nearer to the gentleman.

"We couldn't disturb him if we liked," he said, shaking his head. "Mr Fortescue is dead."

18

"The Lord is my shepherd. I shall not want," intoned Judith.

Louisa-Margaretta was surprised to see not only Mrs Daw but also Miss Sweet and Mr Nightingale joining Judith in one corner of the green room, where they knelt in prayer together.

She shook her head. Judith had been raised in churches, so perhaps it was not surprising that she could say the Lord's Prayer during any trying moment, but Louisa-Margaretta would not have been able to pray for Mr Fortescue. Jesus might have ordered his followers to love their enemies, but that simply confirmed for Louisa-Margaretta that she was not suited to follow Jesus's teachings too closely. Mr Fortescue was gone forever, and she still hated him.

Of course, she was not the only person who had failed to join in. Mr Solier was playing passages from one of his operas at an old instrument.

"Do you have music?" asked Jasper, leaning on the

instrument with a smile. "I could try singing the part that you had in mind for me."

Mr Solier sighed as if the request were a great burden, but he allowed Jasper to take a sheaf of music from the case he carried with him. The role of the young farmer suited Jasper's clear voice perfectly. Though Louisa-Margaretta found that she was still trying to banish the sight of Mr Fortescue's body from her mind, the music helped somewhat. She was never surprised that it was such a wonderful cure for madness.

"Now, then," said Mr Daw. "Dear Miss Byrd. I know there is not much of a kitchen here, but we have a kettle and a fire. Why should we not have a cup of tea?"

"You can make it," she said. "I am hardly a scullery maid."

"No, but you might make the tea with me, in the fashion of a grand hostess," he said. "Come now. There's little else for us to do."

Louisa-Margaretta was able to find one other thing to do. She was starving once again. It felt as if she'd eaten the beefsteak and toasted cheese many weeks ago. Fortunately, Mr Solier's hosts had been thoughtful enough to send a hamper with provisions, and she ate as much as she could of the bread, cheese, dried meat, and even some hothouse fruit. When she had finished, she lay on one of the sofas in the room and drifted off. Though her thoughts were not easy, it was unusual for her to forgo sleep, and she had no intention of doing so that evening. They had little to do but wait, after all. Miss Byrd had sent a neighbor's boy to find one of the Bow Street Runners, and after two young men arrived, one of them had gone to find someone else. One of them was with Mr Fortescue's body in the theatre, and the actors and their assistants were only too happy to retire to the green room.

"May his soul rest in peace," she heard Judith say as she began to wake up. The scent of freshly brewed tea was too appealing to allow her to sleep through the refreshments, especially when it was likely to be much stronger than the terrible stuff Dorothy St Clair had been serving them throughout their visit.

A dark laugh filled the room. "That's a kind-enough thought, Miss St Clair, but I think the fate of his soul is something all of us may imagine," said Mr Nightingale. "Or any of us who have r-r-read Dante Alighieri's work can decide exactly how he is p-passing this night."

Some murmurs followed, but nobody except Judith challenged him.

"That is not for us to judge," said Judith.

Mr Nightingale frowned. "Not j-j-judge his behavior?" he asked. "The man was a menace."

"We may judge that," said Judith. "Indeed, I don't see how any person could ignore it. But it is not for us to decide the fate of his soul."

"Thank heavens for that," murmured Miss Sweet, and the rest of the company laughed.

Mr Daw, who was passing out teacups, nodded in Judith's direction. "You're right enough about that, miss. Make no mistake. But I can only say that Mr Fortescue had few friends in the theatre in spite of his habit of throwing his shillings about."

"Sometimes, he truly threw the coins!" cried Jasper from the piano. "He made a sport of it, throwing the smallest amount of money he could at every stage. He liked to see how little he could give and still see people scramble for it."

Miss Wynn shook her head. "He couldn't just sit in a box

and rattle away, like any other rich man. I think he fancied himself unique."

"Well, good riddance, I say," said Mr Nightingale. "It may be a rather unchristian sentiment, but I'm glad the man is dead."

"Are you?" came a voice from the doorway. "I should be very interested in knowing more about that."

Louisa-Margaretta opened her eyes again.

"Good evening," said Mr Christmas Fudge not unkindly. The man's body was full without being corpulent, and he walked into the room with a small smile. If he had seen Mr Fortescue's body, he made no sign. Louisa-Margaretta was sure he was used to such sights and worse. There were rumors that he was incorruptible, that he had taken the practise of buying protection and turned it on its head.

"I will need to speak to all of you in turn," he said. "Perhaps, Mr St Clair, you might accompany me first?"

It was plainly not a suggestion, and none of the individuals in the room were so foolhardy as to mistake Mr Fudge for an innocent presence. Mr Daw looked down, shaking his head, and Miss Wynn let out an audible gasp.

"Miss Byrd," said Mr Fudge, "perhaps you might direct me to a room where I can speak with Mr St Clair in private."

"Of course," said the director. "We have one very near, though I'm afraid there may still be papers scattered about. Straightaway, sir."

Jasper didn't move right away, instead looking around at his companions as if he might well go anywhere else.

"Mr St Clair," said Mr Fudge as Jasper stood, sweat on his brow. "With me, please."

They went out together, presumably to the room where Judith and Louisa-Margaretta had been working on their revisions. Louisa-Margaretta could hardly tell who was most distressed. Judith was near tears. Before he found his vocation, Jasper St Clair had brought his family their share of trouble. In fact, Judith had privately confessed that she had once been sure he would not come to a good end. Louisa-Margaretta had brothers who had engaged in the same pranks as Jasper St Clair, of course, but they had money and a sterling reputation on their side. When Jasper had turned his considerable talent for impersonation to the business of acting, he no longer had the energy for his old pursuits. And once he'd become a serious singer, he started to be nearly as abstemious as Mr Daw. "I love spirits," he liked to say, "but to keep the spirit of my voice alive, I must decline."

Louisa-Margaretta was not worried about Jasper. No doubt his past brushes with the law would teach him how to conduct himself. But she was scared for Judith.

"I must hear this little conversation," she said. "Miss Byrd probably chose that room for its thin walls. It must have been put in after the theatre was finished."

"It was," said Mr Nightingale, but Mrs Daw shook her head.

"Don't trouble yourself, dear," she said. "It's only a conversation with the magistrate. That Mr Fortescue died here, and now, the gentleman will speak with all of us."

"Yes, and he will get us to say all sorts," said Miss Sweet. "There is no fairness under English law, only the appearance of it."

Something about her pronunciation of the *r* sound was a bit odd to Louisa-Margaretta's ears. Perhaps the poor young girl had forgotten how to articulate because of the shock.

"That is why I must listen," said Louisa-Margaretta. "Judith, you'll come with me."

"Of course," said Judith.

The actors were surprised, but Louisa-Margaretta was

not. Judith disliked fast horses, hunting, and ships—all those things that brought risk to one's person while providing hours of amusement. But when it came to the danger of bringing criminals to justice, Judith was courageous, even reckless at times.

"We shall need a guide," said Louisa-Margaretta. "Where can we listen yet remain unobserved?"

"The prop room," murmured Mrs Daw. "That would be the place. But, girls, this is madness."

Miss Wynn sprang up. "I shall take them," she said.

19

The prop room was piled high with dusty things. Judith was sure they must have done an opera with a nautical theme recently, as there were piles of rope and two little boats that opened at the back. It might be some time before the theatre would attempt such a story again. After all, if many young men were off fighting the French, it would not be considered a matter for cheer.

But she had little time to wonder what Mr Coleman would allow if the war with France dragged on for years, as Mr Fudge had begun asking more serious questions of Jasper. Judith fixed her attention firmly on their conversation.

"Did you know Mr Fortescue?"

Jasper snorted. "Everyone knew him."

"What do you mean by that?" asked Mr Fudge with the balance of strictness and patience common in very experienced governesses.

"He delighted in going about London, feeling superior and causing havoc."

"I see," said Mr Fudge, his voice so low that Judith had to strain to hear. "He caused you some trouble, then?"

"No. But if he was killed, I'm saying it could have been anyone."

"Interesting that you believe he must have been killed."

When Jasper made no answer, the older man continued, "Mr Fortescue appears to have been poisoned. He brought a large hamper full of food with him today, apparently because he wished to stay at the theatre after the members of his club were gone. Be assured that we shall be interviewing his cook at her earliest convenience. However, it is imperative that we speak to any other individuals who were in close proximity to him. That includes you, your fellow thespians, and your guests, all of whom you know well."

Judith trembled. Mr Fudge had not mentioned her by name, but she was terrified that either she or Louisa-Margaretta would be reported for the words they'd had with Mr Fortescue. Louisa-Margaretta, in particular, had never hesitated to tell Mr Fortescue exactly what she thought of him, and she never cared who heard her. If Mr Fudge learned of their arguments, he might think the worst.

Jasper appeared to understand the insinuations and resent them as much as Judith did. "A man like Mr Fortescue must have many enemies."

But none of them were here in the theatre except for us, thought Judith.

"What sort of enemies?" asked Mr Fudge. "And what sort of man was Mr Fortescue?"

"A difficult one," said Jasper.

The silence stretched long enough that Jasper tried to elaborate on his answer.

"Most patrons just pay," he said. "They have no wish to

influence the production itself. But Mr Fortescue was different."

When it became clear that Jasper would not elaborate on that answer without encouragement, Mr Fudge continued, "Why did the Duke of Ormonde not pay for this production? As I recall, he has laid down a great deal of money for many of your operas in the past."

Jasper looked away. "He has had some trouble with his estate. Even now, he says he may have to go back to the country in a matter of days. But he wished to see us in this new opera first."

"Wished to see whom?" said Mr Fudge.

A pause once again followed.

"Justice is the most noble aim," said Mr Fudge gently. "I wish you would consider my question, Mr St Clair."

"You have been listening to gossip," said Jasper.

They heard Mr Fudge's soft tread. Judith wondered whether he was getting close to her cousin, leaning close to Jasper in some strange imitation of intimacy.

"What gossip might that be, then?"

"About the actresses in our production and the Duke of Ormonde. I can assure you both ladies are above reproach."

A tiny sound came from Miss Wynn, and Judith was surprised to see her trying to muffle her reaction. Her face had turned quite pink. Judith attempted not to notice. She was just as embarrassed at the idea of the two ladies fighting for the rich man's favors as anyone directly involved could be.

"I'm sure you feel that everyone here tonight was above reproach," said Mr Fudge. "Otherwise, why would you associate with them?"

But his words were too pointed to be sincere.

"I remember you," said Jasper. "Last time we met, you

made accusations against me that were completely false. You seemed to think I had killed a young woman, and your reasoning didn't make any sense. You got everything wrong."

The longest silence yet followed.

"I got it right in the end, though," said Mr Fudge, seemingly unaffected.

It chilled Judith. Mr Fudge had a reputation not only for being fair but for seeking the truth as well. He managed to solve crimes without evidence and to gain confessions where the most careful criminals should have been certain of success.

Miss Wynn squeezed her hand. Judith was on the verge of tears. She had to remind herself Jasper was not guilty. Because he was innocent, Mr Fudge would not be able to find anything to connect him to the murder.

As soon as she had the thought, she realized it was no comfort to her. People had been wrongly accused of murder in the past, even by Mr Fudge.

Silently, she began to pray.

20

Louisa-Margaretta shook her friend's arm. Judith, like Louisa-Margaretta's mother, seemed to have a talent for praying at the most inconvenient times.

"We have to get out of here, Judith," she said. "Mr Fudge is almost finished with Jasper."

"How do you know?" whispered Miss Wynn.

They could not see well in the dim room, but Louisa-Margaretta could hear the doubt in Miss Wynn's voice.

"I know Mr Fudge," she said, not wishing to lay bare the whole of her family's history with Mr Christmas Fudge.

Judith knew of the many connections between the two old families, but she would never betray Louisa-Margaretta.

Miss Wynn led both ladies out of the prop room and back to the green room, where Mr Nightingale was playing a dirge on the pianoforte, humming along loudly.

"Sit down," said Mrs Daw, forcing Miss Wynn, Judith, and Louisa-Margaretta to take seats next to Miss Sweet, who was beginning to look rather droopy from exhaustion.

They'd left just in time, as Mr Fudge came in with a

mysterious smile, following Jasper as if he were herding the young man.

Jasper made for the corner where Judith was sitting, but with a wary look at Mr Fudge, he changed course and went over to the pianoforte.

If he had been hoping to take the attention away from Judith, he did not succeed. Mr Fudge surprised them all.

"Right," he said. "Mr St Clair ought to escort his guests home. Miss Haddington and Miss St Clair, if you would accompany me, please. I will speak to you now. That way, you may all leave together."

Judith and Louisa-Margaretta followed him, and Louisa-Margaretta could not keep the phrase "lambs to slaughter" from coming to mind. She scowled at Mr Fudge. He would be speaking to her and Judith together for sinister reasons of his own, no doubt.

"I hope you have been well, Miss Haddington, and your brothers," Mr Fudge said. "Please send my best regards to your parents."

Louisa-Margaretta wished she could take comfort from his demeanor. Unfortunately, if he thought she was guilty of the murder, no respect for her or her family would keep him from sending her to the scaffold. On the contrary, he might send her there all the more easily. He might feel that he had been taken in and be eager to make an example of her.

"I have not seen them for some time," she said. "I've been traveling."

Mr Fudge nodded. "Ah yes, to Russia! Many an Englishman has never been close to St Petersburg. It is a very uncommon destination."

When Louisa-Margaretta didn't answer, she could feel Judith hastening to make up for her ill breeding.

"It was a lovely city," said Judith. "Very, erm, very cold, of course."

Louisa-Margaretta took her friend's arm. Poor Judith could hardly speak.

"Do you not wish to speak to us separately, Mr Fudge," she asked, challenging him. It would not be proper for him to speak to a young lady without a chaperone present, but she wondered whether he would trust what he heard from the two of them together.

Mr Fudge gave another small smile. "The two of you are as thick as thieves. I have no doubt that you would share everything with each other, so I see little purpose in a separation. After all, blood is thicker than water."

It was a strange phrase to choose. Louisa-Margaretta wondered if he was thinking of Judith's kinship with Jasper St Clair when he said it and hoped he might be keeping an open mind on the subject of Jasper's culpability. And Judith's honesty, of course. Judith could lie, sometimes very convincingly, but it cost her a great deal to do so.

"Where was Mr Fortescue's hamper?" Mr Fudge asked.

Louisa-Margaretta remembered Mr Fortescue brandishing it at her as he invited her to eat with him, and she felt a small pang of fear before she remembered that he was beyond harming her. The man's secrets had died with him, and while she was trying not to feel triumphant, gratitude kept springing up within her heart.

"He kept the hamper with him," Louisa-Margaretta said. "Once everyone began rehearsing, he sat in front of the stage."

"Who was close enough to slip something into it?" asked Mr Fudge.

"Nobody," said Judith quickly.

Silence followed for a moment.

"Miss St Clair," said Mr Fudge, "I hope you are not speaking out of turn. Are you quite certain that at every moment, no individual approached the place where Mr Fortescue was seated?"

Judith, shamed into silence, made no response.

Louisa-Margaretta glared at Mr Fudge. "I stood near enough to him to put something in it," she said. "And I didn't like him either."

"Miss Haddington!" cried Judith, sending Louisa-Margaretta a warning with her eyes.

Louisa-Margaretta chose to ignore it. "You will not find anyone who liked him," she said stoutly. "I passed most of my time shut away in this very room with Miss St Clair. We had a great deal of work to get through, and we managed."

She looked at the parchment pages scattered about and at the old pianoforte where Judith had picked out the tunes. All of it had passed in an instant. And though Judith had done the lion's share of the work, Louisa-Margaretta had been proud of composing some lines that were really quite clever. *Could someone really have murdered a gentleman while we were sitting here, talking of how best to insert a funeral into the plot of the silly opera?*

There would be a funeral soon. That much was quite certain. Perhaps a rather elaborate one.

"Who inherits?" Louisa-Margaretta asked.

Mr Fudge peered at her. "It is a wise question," he said carefully.

"He had no living relations I can think of and no children." *No legitimate children,* she thought but did not add. Revealing any knowledge of Mr Fortescue's family was foolhardy, but if she were to learn the real culprit, understanding the inheritance would be essential.

Mr Fudge stood. "I'm sure I shall learn more in the

coming days," he said. "And with the size of Mr Fortescue's fortune, even with my private nature, such information is not going to be kept quiet. There is simply too much gossip here in town. In the meantime, ladies, please accompany Mr St Clair to his home."

"Is that all?" asked Louisa-Margaretta. "You kept Mr St Clair talking much longer."

Mr Fudge looked at her with such insight that she was almost certain he knew the conversation with Jasper had not been a private one.

"I cannot think of any other relevant questions for the two of you," said Mr Fudge. "Since I hardly think either of you ladies is likely to be a murderer, the wisest course of action would be for you to both depart and sleep."

Louisa-Margaretta happened to agree, but she was still cross with Mr Fudge for the manner in which he had questioned Jasper and very nearly accused the Lyceum Theatre of harboring a murderer in the cast of *Così fan tutte*.

"Very well, then," she said. "Come, Judith. I'm sure Mr Fudge would like to speak to the others."

And she marched her friend out of the room, not bothering to look back and see whether Mr Fudge had followed.

21

———————

Mr Solier's hosts had insisted he come back to them by carriage, and he offered to take Louisa-Margaretta, Judith, and Jasper back to their home before he retired for the night. It meant that the three of them did have to wait while Mr Fudge spoke with Mr Solier, which he only did after a brief conversation with Miss Sweet and Miss Wynn. The two young ladies were seen separately, but Mrs Daw acted as a sort of chaperone. Judith was not surprised to see they were both distressed by the conversations and also that they would not allow themselves to cry. She also could not conceive of displaying any emotion in front of Mr Fudge, distressing though their conversations had been.

As soon as the four of them were in the privacy of the carriage, Judith took her cousin's hand.

"Oh, Jasper!" she said. "I hope it was not very awful for you."

He let out a deep sigh. "Of course it was awful," he said. "To think it was that dreadful magistrate, Mr Christmas Fudge! And what a name!"

"He is supposed to be very effective in his work," snapped Louisa-Margaretta.

"Hardly a point of pride when one's work is sending men to the scaffold," said Jasper. Then he looked carefully at Mr Solier. "I'm sorry, sir. I speak too hastily."

Mr Solier raised his eyebrows. "When one has known the reality of blood," he said grandly, "speaking of it does very little harm."

Judith didn't challenge Louisa-Margaretta's fiancé, though she thought his statement rather odd. To the best of her knowledge, he had been at a music school in Vienna when a revolution broke out in France. Though he had lost friends and neighbors, his closest family members all managed to escape. But instead of settling with them in Prussia, he had chosen to keep traveling all over Europe, hoping to make a living as a composer.

Mr Solier sighed, resettling himself in the seat. He made no move to comfort Louisa-Margaretta or to seek comfort from her.

"My first English patron gone," he said. "And all the others fail to see the merits of my opera. This country is centuries behind the rest of Europe, and your Mr Coleman will make it worse. How is any composer supposed to write about a serious subject?"

Judith looked down. She thought it best not to point out that Mr Fortescue had agreed to pay for *Così fan tutte* and the production of Mr Solier's comic opera not because he saw value in either performance but because he wanted to maintain a hold over Louisa-Margaretta.

"Perhaps we can find another patron," Judith said gently.

Mr Solier shook his head. "Not an English one, I don't think," he said. "But it is no matter. Here, we have arrived at your little home."

The carriage stopped, and the driver clambered down to help the ladies out, but nobody moved.

"They will never find the killer," said Louisa-Margaretta. "Everyone had reason to kill Mr Fortescue, and the world is better for it."

Judith shot her a sharp look. "Murder is a sin," she said.

"I trust your ecumenical expertise, Judith, but do the Quakers and all of the Church of England clergymen agree on this point?"

"Everyone agrees on it," said Judith, aware that she was flushing. "It is an idea foundational to all religions."

"And a very good one," said Jasper. "Do not distress yourself, Judith. I'm sure Miss Haddington only wishes to remind us that Mr Fortescue was a soldier of sorts."

Mr Solier wrinkled his nose. "A lazy man," he said. "Nothing but money and gambling and gadding about in high society. What sort of soldier is that?"

"One who was at war with the whole world. And now he is a casualty."

22

Louisa-Margaretta was last at the breakfast table the next day. It was, in fact, hardly breakfast, as Dorothy quickly pointed out.

"I'm sorry. The food has all gone cold," she said, not sounding sorry at all. For someone who lived in such close proximity to the theatrical life, Dorothy was an utterly unconvincing actress, though Louisa-Margaretta suspected that was because of indifference and not innate ability. "Perhaps, dear brother, this latest incident will make you reconsider your dedication to that theatre."

Jasper's face showed only traces of discomfort. He was finishing his crumpet and taking sips of pale, watery "tea." "I don't think there is any very safe profession. And Papa no longer requires help with his business interests, not when our brothers are with him."

"Yes, but the theatre is so very difficult," said Dorothy. "You get one decent role, are paid a bit, then have only to find another. How is one supposed to make a living?"

"By living simply," said Jasper.

Judith touched her cousin's arm. "Jasper tells me that

both of you are able to save a portion of his wages by living here," she said. "You must be an excellent housekeeper. I'm sure Aunt Leah would be very proud of your frugality."

Dorothy frowned. "Well, it would not be possible if my father did not send us *some* money. We can afford a life in town better than some of the actors, even if I dream of moving to the country."

"Perhaps someday," said Judith.

Dorothy grabbed the teapot and began pouring tea into a cup for Louisa-Margaretta with graceless movements. "We are not all the recipients of many marriage proposals," she said, giving Louisa-Margaretta a look of such spite that the latter sat at attention. "Miss Haddington, I understand that Mr Fortescue wished to be united in marriage with you."

Jasper shifted in his seat. "Really, Dorothy," he said. "If Miss Haddington does not wish to discuss such a topic—"

"Nothing could be further from the truth," Louisa-Margaretta lied, interrupting Jasper's poor attempts to make up for his sister's ill-breeding. "Oh, it's certainly possible that I once caught his eye, though it did not end in a proposal. But of late, he was more than pleased to pay for the production in order to help my dear fiancé make his London debut."

Judith didn't appear nearly as nervous as Jasper, but she also plainly wished to cut off Dorothy's rude speculations. "Perhaps Mr Solier wishes to be considered a patron of the arts. Maybe it is due to vanity, but such impulses are not uncommon among men in his position."

Dorothy smiled, clearly not taken in by either explanation. "Miss Haddington, I'm sure Mr Solier will be pleased to learn that it was for your sake that Mr Fortescue laid down his money, not because of any appreciation of his art."

She put a steaming teacup in front of Louisa-Margaretta, who did not touch it.

"If you spread such lies, I shall deny all of them," Louisa-Margaretta said.

Judith began, "I'm sure there is no need—"

Louisa-Margaretta stood. "My fiancé's operas are not fully appreciated in London, but I am prodigiously proud of them," she announced. "And as my parents will soon be arriving in London for the wedding, I must begin to think of my trousseau."

She went back to the room she was sharing with Judith to gather her things for going out. As her money was limited, she might not be able to make the purchases she would like, but she could wait for her parents' arrival and get a sense of her desires while doing so. And she was determined to have a fine new dress made for the express purpose of irritating Dorothy St Clair.

Judith came in only a moment later. "My cousins are our hosts."

It was as near to a reproach as one was likely to hear from Judith, and it irritated Louisa-Margaretta still more for its careful phrasing.

"I do not see why Dorothy should try to ruin my prospects simply because she has none of her own," said Louisa-Margaretta. "Is not your uncle rich? She could live with any of her brothers or at least marry a fortune hunter."

Judith considered. "Dorothy seems more attuned to the dangers of a mercenary marriage than she once was. Though she wishes to live in grand style in the country, she wants to do so as someone with a position in the household, not having to take her place behind a sister-in-law. If she lived with one of her brothers, she would be seen as a sad spinster, a hanger-on. I daresay we both know what that is like."

Louisa-Margaretta pulled a shawl about her shoulders hastily. Though the summer day had been hot, rain was threatening, but she was determined to go forth on her outing. "And why are you going on about mercenary marriages, Judith? I have the fortune and Mr Solier, the genius. So in some respects, we are equal."

Judith shook her head. "I'm hardly in a position to give anyone advice on that subject. As you know, Morgan's resources are certainly larger than mine. But I'm concerned that we may outstay our welcome here, Louisa-Margaretta. Could you apologize to my cousins, please?"

Louisa-Margaretta shook her head. "I make no objection to anything you may say on my behalf, but I must see to my trousseau. Don't expect me to return anytime soon."

"Could you help me speak to someone else about Morgan?" asked Judith.

Louisa-Margaretta could see that it cost Judith to make the request, but she was too cross with the St Clairs to honour it. "No. And I won't listen to any more about you gadding about between London and Vienna on your own, either. What foolishness!"

Judith looked away, her lip beginning to tremble, but Louisa-Margaretta marched out.

23

———

Judith took some moments to compose herself. She knew she would have to answer for her friend's behavior, and it pained her to be left to do so yet again. Louisa-Margaretta had been instructed in the rules of politeness and decorum but seemed determined to disregard them. Sometimes, she was a surprisingly attentive friend, making up for her rudeness with a generosity of spirit that always surprised Judith. Other times, Louisa-Margaretta appeared just as spoiled as any tiny child.

"Your Miss Haddington was in high dudgeon this morning," said Jasper when Judith emerged from her room. "She has the temperament for opera, all the dramatics and noise. And the bit where one storms offstage rather than speak to an 'enemy.' Perhaps she will make Mr Solier a good wife."

Judith, ashamed for her friend, corrected him. "Louisa-Margaretta will certainly make him a proper wife. And I am sorry for her rudeness."

"You spoil her," said Dorothy. "If her friends did not tolerate such behavior, she would learn to think before speaking."

Judith made some assenting murmurs, though Dorothy was not correct on that point. She had seen Louisa-Margaretta face unpleasant consequences before, yet her friend had learned very little. Miss Haddington would always be a lady who leapt first and looked later.

"Well," said Dorothy, "I suppose now you won't be working, brother."

Jasper looked down. "I'm going out," he said. "As to whether I will be working, I can ask Miss Byrd. If anyone can find a way to rescue this opera, I hope she can."

Dorothy looked longingly after her brother as he prepared to leave. "I suppose I shall see what Sarah has planned for our dinner. She was late again, and things have been so dear at the market. Everyone thinks we're to be invaded at any moment, and for some reason, they seem to think making more purchases is the way to survive such an eventuality."

She sat without making the slightest of movements, and Judith felt her heart going out to the young woman. Dorothy was constantly complaining that their hired girl was late or that she hadn't come on a day she was meant to be there. Judith had begun to suspect that Sarah's wages were aligned with very limited hours and that the sweet young girl was only present at the St Clair household rather irregularly. Perhaps they shared her services with another family.

"Let's tidy some of this up ourselves," said Judith. "Then perhaps you could accompany me on a call."

Dorothy came alive again at once. "Whom are we to visit?"

Judith pretended not to notice the way her cousin's face fell when she heard the answer.

"Mr Christmas Fudge and his family."

Dorothy sniffed. "Into the lion's den, then."

Judith blinked, trying to collect her nerves. "Yes. I'm afraid it must be done."

24

They received a warm welcome at the home of Mr Fudge. The man himself was present, which was Judith's sincerest hope. He had a reputation for doing much of his work in the study of his stately home.

"We must sit down to tea," said Mr Fudge after Judith had introduced her cousin. He showed them to an ornate sitting room, where a gentleman rose to greet them and two ladies appeared surprised by their arrival.

"May I present my mother-in-law, Mrs Stone, my son, Felton, and my daughter, Frances."

"And I'll be presenting myself" came a deep voice from the corner. "I'm his niece."

Mrs Stone spoke sharply to the young woman. "That's quite enough, Jenny."

Mr Fudge looked discomfited, which was surprising to Judith. "I cannot think how I did not see you. Of course. Well, so it is. We are all here."

The young woman, Jenny, nodded to Judith and Dorothy. "You're related to that Jasper St Clair, then? We all saw him in that opera two months ago, the one with all the ships. He sings well enough. I told Granny I wanted to leave in the first interval, but she wouldn't let me, so I slept through most of it. Your Mr St Clair was better than that woman he was supposed to be in love with. And she was an old goat!"

Judith pursed her lips, wishing she had brought Louisa-Margaretta instead of her cousin. But to her surprise, Dorothy burst into musical laughter.

"Yes, his love interest was a lady about twenty years older," she said. "I'm afraid they did not suit. Jasper did not do a very good impression of being enamoured with her."

Mr Felton Fudge looked at Dorothy, his eyes shining. "Do you act as well, then, Miss St Clair?"

Judith thought her cousin might be offended, as most society families still thought it rather scandalous for a woman to act. But she seemed flattered, perhaps happy to have been asked.

"Oh no," she said. "I do not have my brother's talent. And I'm not terribly fond of London. I much prefer the country."

"Do you?" asked Mr Felton Fudge.

Judith was half tempted to tell them both about some of the very serious disadvantages of country living. Instead, she made use of the moment to move away from her cousin and the two Fudge children. Under the pretext of inspecting the view from the large windows at the front of the room, she ensured that she was closer to Mr Fudge.

"Mr Fudge," she said. "Last night, you said that justice was the most noble aim one could ever consider."

His eyes were piercing. "I do not recall saying that to *you*, Miss St Clair."

Judith looked away, but in order to lie convincingly, she had to meet Mr Fudge's gaze. "My friend Miss Haddington is not the only person who shares her thoughts and experiences with me, Mr Fudge."

She remembered those moments in the prop room, crouching next to the wall to eavesdrop. She would have to take special care not to repeat anything else from that conversation to Mr Fudge.

"Well," he said, "I would agree with you. I'm afraid it puts you in a rather awkward position, Miss St Clair."

"It does not," said Judith.

"It does," said Jenny.

Since nobody had yet used her last name, it was impossible to know how to address her. She had not yet outgrown the age when a young person thought every controversial thought they had was strikingly original and must be given a hearing.

"One of your friends done it," she said, slouching in her chair. "It's rather awkward, that."

The older woman, Mrs Stone, gave her a reproachful glare. "One ought never to make any assumptions, dear."

"Yes, but nobody else was there, were they, Uncle Christmas?" Jenny said. "So it isn't much of an assumption."

Mr Fudge looked away. "One of the three actors is a murderer," he said. "I would shield you from this if I could, Miss St Clair. But this information is essential for your own safety. You, Miss Dorothy St Clair, and Miss Haddington all must avoid that place until we find the culprit."

"That is also an assumption," said his mother-in-law softly, but he ignored her.

"I hardly think any of us would be in danger," said Judith. "We were not intimately connected with Mr Fortescue."

"But you may have been witnesses unwittingly," said Mr

Fudge. "You may not be aware of what you know. Do not think of going to the theatre. I must urge you."

"It's devilish dull much of the time anyway," said young Jenny, and Mrs Stone frowned at her.

"There's no great harm in going occasionally, but it is best not to become involved with any of the actors," Mrs Stone said. "Theatrical persons have more than their fair share of sin and immorality."

Judith waited for some softening or perhaps an apology. She thought the woman might say something like, "Meaning no offense, Miss St Clair. Your cousin is an excellent young man."

But she said no such thing.

"This is rather grim," said Jenny, though she didn't look displeased. "Let's speak of something more appropriate, shall we? Did I say all that right, then, Granny? Are you quite convinced?"

The old woman looked as if she were trying not to laugh. "Well enough, but I must wait to see what topic you raise. You have a habit of choosing an even worse subject when you attempt to turn the conversation."

"How about courtship? That's safe enough," said the young woman. "Everyone thinks my cousin Felton jilted that Miss Nicholson, but I was the only one who could tell he never cared for her in the first place."

Judith started. She glanced over at Mr Felton Fudge, but he was still speaking to Dorothy and had not noticed the slight.

"I'll try again," said Jenny. She was the only person laughing, though Judith thought Louisa-Margaretta would have loved the irreverent aside. "Miss St Clair, have you got yourself an eligible beau?"

Judith looked down. She would normally obscure her

story, but it occurred to her that the Fudge family was one of the few she had not yet asked for help.

"My fiancé went missing," she said. "He was accompanying another gentleman back from the Congress of Vienna. I suppose you heard."

For the first time, the young woman looked chastened. "Well, that's terrible luck. He was with that viscount chap, then? I'm very sorry for him."

Mrs Stone nodded in sympathy. "I am also very sorry for your loss, Miss St Clair."

"We aren't sure what became of any of them," said Judith boldly. "So I'm hoping that some member of our government will see fit to send out a search party."

Miss Felton had just taken a seat closer to her grandmother, and she stared at Judith. "In the middle of a war?"

"Perhaps this is the best time," said Judith, her tone faltering. "Everyone is so concerned about Napoleon Bonaparte that nobody will notice a small party going off from England to Vienna."

"And avoiding France entirely?" asked Mr Fudge. "My dear, I'm very sorry, but it can't be done. And if the powers that be had any interest in searching for the lost gentlemen, it would have been done long ago."

Judith bristled. She hated that Mr Fudge didn't include himself in his description of the powerful. He had just as much influence as any member of Parliament, if only he would use it.

"I would go with you," said Jenny, who had recovered her composure and sense of humour. "But one of these Fudges would follow me and kill me, so I'm afraid I would slow your journey. But I'm sure I could lend you a very good knife. You might be needing it."

Judith looked at her with some interest. Of all of the

people in the room, only the uncouth young woman had appeared to understand that Judith was entirely prepared to go herself. She feared failure more than she worried for her life, so she had not yet gone, but she would have to consider it.

"If you cannot help me, Mr Fudge, I will keep consulting other gentlemen," said Judith. "But as I'm sure you can imagine, it is a difficult task. In fact, we have very little time to spare."

She nodded, gazing at her cousin, but Dorothy did not notice the signal.

"Cousin," said Judith pointedly, "I'm afraid I have forgotten the time. I'm sure the family must be getting on."

Dorothy's expression was crestfallen, and Judith suffered a pang of guilt. The young girl who had lived for every ball was gone, replaced by a spinster who hoped only for an afternoon with her cousin's friend's acquaintances. What a fall from grace, indeed. Judith reminded herself to pray later that more fun and friendship might become a part of Dorothy's life once more.

"I'm sorry. I would not wish to trouble you or overstay my welcome," said Dorothy. "But it has been a lovely visit! I cannot remember the last time I passed such an enjoyable afternoon."

It had hardly been an afternoon. In fact, the visit had been very short, but Judith gave a half smile. "Quite. Thank you for being such gracious hosts. Please don't trouble yourselves. We can see ourselves out."

25

"I'm not sure I like this fashion," said Louisa-Margaretta, looking at a gown that had so many ribbons it must have been weighed down by them. "Aren't these little ribbons always getting in the way of things?"

The shopkeeper pursed her lips. "Well, madam, unless one is constantly moving about, I would hardly call them much of an inconvenience."

Louisa-Margaretta's third-best gown had gotten rather shabby during their time in Russia, and she had not thought to wear her best one when she wanted to look about in the shops. But the result seemed to be that shopkeepers believed she could not afford a decent trousseau. Louisa-Margaretta, used to the utmost deference from people in all lines of business, did not appreciate the disrespect.

Sure enough, the shopkeeper was quick enough to point out Louisa-Margaretta's distinct lack of funds.

"Would you like to place an order now, madam?" she asked.

Louisa-Margaretta looked about, wishing that the place were more crowded.

"Perhaps I shall look for a moment more," she said. "I must say it is strange that there aren't more customers today."

The woman's expression went sour. "It's this war. For some reason, all Londoners seem to think that purchasing fine muslin would be some sort of affront to the men going up against that dirty Corsican. Why, I couldn't say."

"Well, your muslin is indeed quite fine," said Louisa-Margaretta. "But even in wartime, people must have something to wear."

"Indeed," said the woman. But Louisa-Margaretta had not succeeded in winning her over. "I've got to eat in wartime, as well, and pay for these materials. So if you were not thinking of making a purchase today—"

Louisa-Margaretta heard a noise over her shoulder as a gentleman and a lady entered the small shop.

"You're here again!" said the woman.

"You have the finest fabrics outside of Paris, my dear," someone said loudly. "And our Miss Sweet deserves only the best."

Louisa-Margaretta stood rooted to the spot. She was wearing a large hat, and a glance told her that Miss Sweet had not recognised her. Rather, she was on the arm of the Duke of Ormonde, laughing and looking at him with adoration.

"You do spoil me, dear," she said. "We were here only last week!"

Louisa-Margaretta pointed at a fine but dark dress pinned to a mannequin near the back of the store.

"This one," she whispered to the shopkeeper's assistant,

a young girl who scarcely looked older than ten. "Let me try it on, please."

It looked near enough her size, so she hoped the request would not be suspicious.

The young girl took her to one of the rooms where the ladies could change, helping Louisa-Margaretta on with the dress as if it were second nature. Louisa-Margaretta, who usually had a great deal to say when purchasing clothing, listened in absolute silence as Miss Sweet spoke with the duke.

"You should have bought me something for the coming weeks, my dear," she teased. "You know I have nothing black. It doesn't suit me. I'm too fair."

The man laughed. "We should buy this beautiful pink dress to mark the occasion! One cannot be too celebratory, my dear. Mr Fortescue was nothing more than vermin, and we ought to all be thankful that he is out of our way. Isn't that true, Mrs. Norman?"

The shopkeeper tut-tutted. "Well, I'm not usually one to speak ill of a gentleman who settles his account on time. So many don't, I'm afraid! But I did not like your Mr Fortescue. Whenever he came here, it was to buy fine things for some lady or another. He needed a wife."

Louisa-Margaretta looked at herself in the flattering deep-blue gown. Even in the dimly lit space, she could see that it looked very well on her. And she certainly would not have enough money to afford it. Still, she smiled at the young girl and asked for help getting back into her ordinary gown, expressing great admiration for the new fashion.

"I can't think of a woman who'd want to spend any length of time with him," said the duke.

"Or any man," twittered Miss Sweet. "He was giving me

so much trouble at the theatre. If you had been there, I'm afraid you would have challenged him."

The duke laughed again. "Oh, I have never been one for dueling, as you know. But for you, my love, anything!"

Miss Sweet gave an unladylike snort. "You would have had nothing to fear from Mr Fortescue. I'm sure he wished to keep you alive."

"Indeed," said the duke. "Always threatening me with the vilest slander. I refused to give him money, but I should have seen him banished."

For the first time, the man sounded genuinely upset, and Louisa-Margaretta could hear Miss Sweet trying to calm him.

"The pink dress is lovely," she said. "But perhaps I shall come another day for the fitting. Miss Byrd will be wanting me at the theatre."

"Of course," said the shopkeeper, who was very gracious. "And I could make a simple black one for you if you would like. The material would be fine but with little adornment."

The duke said no to this, but Miss Sweet assented.

"We never know when we will lose someone genuinely dear to us," she said. "So I ought to have something if I must wear full mourning someday, my love. And as for Mr Fortescue's funeral, well, this would be little more than a costume. And I would only be wearing it if I watched the procession from the street. It doesn't much signify what any woman wears on the day."

"Very well," said the duke. "I do not object if that is your desire, my dear."

They said their farewells, and just when Louisa-Margaretta thought it would be safe to come out, the duke came back in.

"Mrs. Norman, another black dress if you please, for Miss Wynn," he said. "She may need it for the same reason."

Louisa-Margaretta turned away from the young girl. She had assumed there was some truth to the rumours of the duke favoring first Miss Wynn then Miss Sweet. But that was shocking, even to her.

"Would you like the dress, miss?" asked the young girl, beginning to look doubtful while maintaining a polite and professional tone.

The shopkeeper's statement about Mr Fortescue settling his accounts had reminded Louisa-Margaretta of something.

"Yes," she said, hoping her tone was definitive. She stepped out, and to the disapproving Mrs Norman, she said that she would pick up the gown as soon as it might be ready for her.

"And will you be paying now, Miss?" asked the woman. She was clearly taking care to be polite yet attentive.

"No," Louisa-Margaretta said. "Please put it on the account of Mrs and Mr Ambrose Haddington, my parents. They can settle it when they arrive here in London."

At once, the woman's expression changed. "Why, you must be Miss Haddington, then! I am so sorry I didn't recognise you. It has been at least a year since you were here."

Louisa-Margaretta smiled sadly. Apparently, she still required someone else's name in order to get the respect to which she was entitled.

"Yes," she said. "I have been out of the country. And with any luck, I shall leave again very soon."

26

Louisa-Margaretta arrived back at the St Clair household having visited several shops and ordered several beautiful gowns. She had always liked the idea of collecting items she might bring to a marriage. When she had been eager to marry Isaac, there wasn't time for such a thing. She had shot from a young lady with no interest in courtship into a woman running to the altar. After her parents removed her from that engagement, deeming the alliance with a young man from a well-known Jewish family unsuitable, Louisa-Margaretta had taken no interest in the subject of matrimony for years after, so she collected nothing. Even when men were courting her, she had never quite been able to summon up the enthusiasm she used to feel for a wedding as the mark of a new life. Her own lack of skill in the area of embroidery, of course, also left her with only fine linens that had been prepared by others.

And though she had a good bit of her trousseau prepared for her marriage to Ivo Solier, she still felt empty. Thankful that Judith and her cousin had not returned, she moved about the little sitting room with languor and distaste for the arrangements. Judith's uncle's wealth allowed Jasper and Dorothy St Clair to have more space and privacy than they otherwise could have afforded. She struggled to think of how their quarters would look without this flow of extra money.

She was interrupted by the arrival of Mr Solier, who came to her with a command.

"You must change my opera," he said. "I have already spoken to Miss Byrd this morning, and she has a sense of the things your Mr Coleman will not accept. These English censors!"

"He is not *my* Mr Coleman," said Louisa-Margaretta. Her own fiancé was talking about the difficult old man as if he were some kind of beau. "I detest that gentleman."

"But you have enough knowledge of his tastes to fix this," said Mr Solier, pursing his lips.

"Dear Ivo." It was strange how his Christian name still felt unfamiliar to her, though they had been engaged for months. "This is a great deal of work."

He moved closer to her, leaning in as if to kiss her.

For Mr Solier, that was unusual. He had only kissed her twice their entire engagement, though Louisa-Margaretta supposed it was largely because they were never alone together. Someone else was always with them, which Louisa-Margaretta told herself was a necessary protection to preserve her reputation and keep her from being tempted by lust.

But when he did kiss her, the coldness of the embrace struck her. It was like kissing a statue. There was nothing in particular wrong with him, but the moment held no drop of passion.

"Not before we are married," she said, pulling away from

him with a teasing smile. If she was not mistaken, he looked somewhat relieved.

"Very well," he said. "And when is that to be?"

It was a simple-enough question, but without knowing when her parents would arrive in London, Louisa-Margaretta couldn't answer it.

"Soon enough," she said. "My parents will be happy to purchase any license I request."

She changed the subject back to his opera, looking at the papers he'd brought with him.

"You ought to do it yourself," she said. "How am I to know exactly how to change it?"

"I could hardly take a knife to my child," said Mr Solier. "I would not be surprised if I bled, to make such changes without regard for art."

He caressed the pages, looking pained at the very thought.

And Louisa-Margaretta couldn't help but wonder how he would treat his actual child, were he ever to be so blessed. *Would he love the babe with the same tenderness he shows for his music or shove it aside in favor of the joys of composition?*

She was saved replying by Judith and Dorothy, who came in without the rosy cheeks that Louisa-Margaretta would have expected in the cold weather.

"Are you not cold?" she asked them.

"Mr Felton Fudge took us back in his carriage," said Dorothy, her grin as wide as Louisa-Margaretta had ever seen it. "He simply would not allow us to walk."

Not usually one to feel pity for those without means, Louisa-Margaretta nevertheless felt a pang of sorrow. Poor Dorothy St Clair, with circumstances so straightened that even a very short carriage ride was London's greatest gift.

"Well," said Louisa-Margaretta, "now we have another opera to fix for the censors, Judith. We should really go to the theatre and see what Miss Byrd needs from us today."

Judith sighed. "I'm afraid our visit to the Fudge family was not entirely successful," she said. "I cannot find a single person in London willing to stand up for your cousin."

Louisa-Margaretta touched her fingers to her temples. "And I am very sorry for that, Judith, but we must still play out the play, in the words of the Bard."

"We shall not play out anything if your horrible censor has his say," said Mr Solier.

"And of course, we require a patron," said Judith. "But truly, dear Morgan's life—"

They were interrupted again by a knock at the door. Dorothy bounded over, and Louisa-Margaretta frowned at the way the young woman had to greet and announce her own guests. It was most undignified.

"Mr Beecham, Mr Cartwright, and Mr Hartsock," she said. "Goodness, but it is a day for company."

27

"I certainly hope our company is not unwelcome," said Mr Beecham with a shrewd look at Judith and Louisa-Margaretta.

Judith hoped he couldn't tell they had been quarreling.

"I was just speaking to my friend about her cousin," she said. Something kept her from adding that Morgan was her fiancé. It seemed easier, in that company, to simply refer to him as a member of Louisa-Margaretta's family. "Mr Morgan Ramsbury has been missing since he left the Congress of Vienna."

"Oh, with those other chaps, wasn't it?" asked Mr Beecham. "Yes, very sad, that. And what's happening in France! And poor Mr Fortescue, of course."

Mr Hartsock frowned. "I'm not sure we should pretend those are all of equal weight, Beecham."

"Mr Fortescue was a liar," snapped Mr Cartwright. "He was a cheat, and I'm sure this young lady's cousin was no such thing."

Judith trembled to hear Morgan referred to in the past

tense. She always refused to speak of him that way. *Such disrespect for one still living!* And she felt certain that he *was* still living, that she would have somehow sensed his demise. Though her certainty was beginning to show a chip here and there, like an old walking stick, in the face of all the many gentlemen who seemed quite sure that Morgan was dead.

They also seemed quite preoccupied with their own affairs, so much so that not one of them noticed Judith's discomfort.

"The solution to that, which you never seemed to hear, was not to play cards with the man," said Mr Beecham sternly.

Mr Cartwright only glared, but Mr Hartsock warmed to the subject. "Indeed, one ought never to do anything with Mr Fortescue. He could always shoot more birds than I could manage, win much more at cards, and sing more tunefully. He was exceptional in every area."

Judith was immediately suspicious. "I have heard few men praise him in that way," she said.

Mr Beecham smiled. "We must always make allowance for family ties," he said. "Mr Hartsock is a distant cousin of Mr Fortescue's. His nearest living relative, I believe."

He didn't need to be any more specific. Judith looked over at Louisa-Margaretta, who was still speaking with her fiancé. They had both been wondering for days who the recipient of Mr Fortescue's wealth would be. They had thought it would be a stranger, if any relation could be found. Since Mr Fortescue's father didn't have English roots, they hadn't been sure whether anyone could be traced through his mother's line.

"Was Mr Fortescue a very attentive relation, then?"

Judith asked Mr Hartsock. She shifted on the settee, uncomfortable under Mr Beecham's probing gaze.

"Well, he had a great tendency to fall out with family members," said Mr Hartsock, blinking and looking down. "So I tried not to provoke him. But after we both joined the same society, we saw a bit more of each other."

"Ah yes, the Beefsteak Club," said Louisa-Margaretta, her lips curling in amusement. "Your beefsteak, I am sorry to say, was of very ordinary quality."

Mr Beecham refused to respond to the teasing.

"Tell me of your own relations, Miss St Clair," said Mr Beecham. "You have your cousins here, but where are your parents?"

"My mother is in heaven," said Judith.

"I am very sorry to hear that," said Mr Beecham.

Judith waved his condolences away. "It happened many years ago now."

He frowned. "But that does not make it easier, of course."

Judith paused. He was speaking as if he understood her pain.

"It does not," she said. "Though I fancy I'm more able to live alongside the grief than I was at first. My friend played no small part in that."

She gazed at Louisa-Margaretta, who had left their circle and was speaking animatedly with Mr Solier. She wondered what the argument was about.

"I am an orphan," said Mr Beecham. "It is the reason for my spectacular rise in politics, but I would give up the career in an instant if I could have a complete family again."

Judith suppressed an impulse to smile. Mr Beecham was not known for his modesty, and while he was absolutely correct that he had been part of an impressive rise, another man would not have put it in the same way. His admission of his reasoning touched her, and she gave a sympathetic nod.

"Perhaps you will have a new family of your own someday," she said. "If you choose to have children, they will not replace your parents, but you can honor their legacy in that manner."

"Yes," Mr Beecham said, and his smile was rather too wide.

Judith noticed too late that Mr Cartwright and Mr Hartsock had abandoned them. Mr Cartwright was trying to engage everyone in a game of cards. Dorothy was grinning, protesting without really seeming to mind, but Louisa-Margaretta appeared quite put out. She was also not looking at Mr Solier, though the two were seated directly beside each other.

"I had better go and play hostess," said Judith shortly.

"Wait," said Mr Beecham. "Miss St Clair, if you would. I would like to speak again about the future of my family."

Judith's cheeks burned. She forced herself to meet Mr Beecham's eyes.

"You have been very honest about your career," she said. "And in truth, it is too demanding to allow for a family."

He laughed, plainly not believing her at all. "Every king, every leader in Parliament has had a wife and children. Well, almost all of them, at any rate."

"But not every queen," said Judith.

"I hardly think I would be considered for that position," said Mr Beecham, his eyes twinkling.

Judith's chest constricted. "Men are able to have wives and children, no matter what their position, because it is considered irrelevant whether they fulfill their obligations," she said. "Women are not."

Mr Beecham gave his easy smile again. "I'm sure I

should not wish to be neglectful of anyone. And I might be able to make certain sacrifices, for the right wife and children, of course."

Judith saw that the rest of the room was observing their conversation, having given up their debate over cards.

She could not bear it.

"I wish you the best of luck, Mr Beecham," she said. "I saw during my mother's lifetime that supporting a husband in his work is no easy task. After she died, I was forced to help my father a great deal with the parish. My sister does it now, of course."

"That is interesting," said Mr Beecham. "But let us speak again of my own future."

"I expect you shall be very busy with the war," said Judith shortly.

Louisa-Margaretta, smiling, began to approach Judith and Mr Beecham. "Speaking of the war again, are we, Judith? I'm sure it is hardly the right sort of subject for a drawing room."

"Dear Louisa-Margaretta, as I said earlier, may we not go to the theatre?"

"War is an excellent reason to marry in haste," said Mr Beecham.

Dorothy giggled as Mr Hartsock said, "Hear! Hear!"

"Louisa-Margaretta," said Judith, raising her voice as much as she could bear. "We must leave!"

With a sigh, Louisa-Margaretta said, "We must go back to the theatre to convince them not to cancel these productions. Now that Mr Fortescue is gone and with him the promise of funds, I'm sure Miss Byrd will see to it that poor Mr Solier's little opera is cancelled."

Judith noticed that her friend did not seem at all upset

about the prospect. "It would be a great disappointment for your fiancé," she chided her.

Louisa-Margaretta's voice was devoid of sympathy. "Really, my dear," she said, lowering her voice so that Mr Solier would not hear. "If he were half as serious about his compositions as he pretends, just writing them would be enough. He wouldn't care whether they were performed."

"Well, I say," said Mr Beecham. He shifted, clearly not comfortable criticizing a fellow gentleman.

"Neither of us would know anything about that," said Judith. "We compose music but do not see ourselves as composers."

Louisa-Margaretta smiled, her annoyance with Judith already gone from her face. "But don't you see, Judith? That is just the difference! We do write music, but we don't pretend that this act is the only thing that gives our lives value. Nobody would think that way but a man. Don't you agree, Mr Beecham?"

Mr Beecham rubbed his neck. "Well, not having either the ambition or the talent, I really cannot say. My friend Hartsock is the only one with such ideas, although I suppose he has not written any operas as of yet. He plans to, I know."

As if on cue, all three of them looked at Mr Hartsock. He was in the corner with Mr Cartwright, Dorothy, and Mr Solier, dealing out cards. Dorothy was leaning away from the cards as if they might harm her, Mr Cartwright was practically touching his hand already, and Mr Solier was shrugging. It was hardly an ideal gathering.

"Well, tell Mr Hartsock if he needs any assistance with writing an opera, he ought to come to Judith and me first," said Louisa-Margaretta. "We have practically rewritten Mr

Mozart's opera, so I suppose it would be a bit of a shame if it were not performed."

"Yes," said Judith, seizing that moment. "It would be a great shame. I'm so sorry, Mr Beecham. You will excuse us."

And without delay, they headed for the Lyceum Theatre.

28

When they found Miss Byrd, she was with a man they didn't recognise. From the tenor of their argument, Louisa-Margaretta guessed at first that they were on intimate terms, but as soon as she saw the face of the man, she knew the two must be related. Though he had a large belly, his face had the same narrow features as the younger woman's. Miss Byrd stiffly introduced the man as her father.

"Pleased to meet you, Mr Byrd," said Louisa-Margaretta. "What brings you here today?"

He laughed, perhaps surprised by her direct approach. "I own the theatre," he said. "But my daughter runs it. And it seems she is rather in need of funds."

Miss Byrd's ears burned red. "*I* am not in need of funds," she snapped. "A man died here. It was rotten luck, but we shall have wasted all our efforts on this opera if we cannot go on without him."

"There is no guarantee Mr Coleman will let you get on at all," said Mr Byrd. "I understand you ladies made a few changes, but it is also quite possible he will not like the piece by this French fellow."

"My fiancé is a French exile," snapped Louisa-Margaretta. "He has every reason to hate Napoleon Bonaparte."

Mr Byrd held up his hands. "I'm quite sorry, Miss Haddington. I meant no offense. But I cannot believe that all the theatregoers will be able to see the nuance in his position. They may simply see France as our enemy and therefore wish to avoid anything created by a Frenchman."

"Then they are fools," said Louisa-Margaretta.

Mr Byrd shrugged. "I never claimed to believe otherwise, though I suppose I shouldn't say it out loud. There are many things theatregoers do and believe that are systematically illogical. For example—"

"Papa," said Miss Byrd firmly.

Louisa-Margaretta could see that Mr Byrd was the sort of man who would happily go on about one of his pet subjects, regardless of the feelings or reactions of those around them. Indeed, her anger tended to show quite plainly on her face, and that was usually enough to cow most of her listeners.

Mr Byrd seemed utterly insensible of her feelings, and Miss Byrd hastened to explain the trouble to Louisa-Margaretta. "Mr Coleman holds all the power here. He could approve your revisions in a moment, but I have no way of making him do so."

"Oh, I can tell you exactly how," said Louisa-Margaretta. "I can visit him if you need such a thing, but you'd be better off taking Miss Sweet or Miss Wynn. Let him explain to a pretty actress why he is denying her the ability to put food on her table."

Mr Byrd shook his head. "Why, Miss Haddington, Mr

Coleman is quite serious, and I'm afraid the plight of an actress, though it may garner his sympathy, is hardly likely to factor into his thinking."

Miss Byrd gave Louisa-Margaretta a shrewd look. "I believe it might, Papa," she said. "After all, both the ladies are convincing actresses under all circumstances. And Mr Coleman is a gentleman, so he will feel that he cannot give them undue consideration, but I'm quite sure he will not be willing to snub them to their faces."

Mr Byrd made for the door. "It is an improper thought," he grumbled. "Mrs Daw would be nearer Mr Coleman's age."

Miss Byrd finally smiled. "Mrs Daw would convince that man to do anything," she said. "Best of all, she would make him think he was acting of his own accord. Yes, perhaps I should bring her along too."

All the talk of pretty faces gave Louisa-Margaretta another idea. Judith would hate it, but it would ensure that the opera was performed.

"There is one of the gentlemen in that Beefsteak Club who might be able to fund at least half a week of performances," she said. "His name is Mr Beecham, and he is an old friend of my family. Perhaps Miss St Clair and I could speak to him about it."

Miss Byrd's shoulders sagged. "That would be marvelous. Everyone knows of Mr Beecham, of course. His reputation is much better than Mr Fortescue's, and he seems rather a favorite with anyone who has dealings with Parliament. I was beginning to think this production was cursed, but if we can only run it for a few days, I know we shall quickly sell enough tickets to make up the costs."

Louisa-Margaretta began to grin. "Why, surely you don't believe in curses?"

Miss Byrd's face remained serious. "Everyone in the theatre believes in curses. We'd be fools not to."

Louisa-Margaretta frowned. "Wouldn't you be, well, rather freer if you put no stock in such things? For example, if I decided to whistle—"

"Don't," said Miss Byrd sharply. "You have no idea what the consequences would be."

Louisa-Margaretta laughed. "What? Did Mr Fortescue whistle before his untimely demise?"

"One doesn't need to whistle," said Miss Byrd. "If there is only a ghost of a rumor that someone has been whistling, actors will forget themselves, half the set pieces will go missing, and someone in the audience will reliably be the worst drunkard we have seen in years. Trust me, Miss Haddington. You may feel you know all about this, but you have very little experience in the theatre. Ask Mr St Clair if you don't believe me."

Louisa-Margaretta shook her head. "You needn't convince me, Miss Byrd. Only get those lovely actresses to convince Mr Coleman, and all shall be well. I promise."

Miss Byrd blinked. "I wish I could trust such a promise."

Louisa-Margaretta smiled. "I'm cleverer than I look, if you can believe it. But if you won't be needing me, I should go find Judith. We must look our best when the show opens, and she has no suitable gowns at all."

29

———

Judith woke the next morning with a troubled conscience. She realised that in spite of Mr Fortescue's death, she had been enjoying her time at the theatre. Rewriting the opera was invigorating, and the way the actors carried on backstage intrigued her. It was as if the theatre were another country, complete with its own form of dress, rituals, and language. She had enjoyed watching Miss Sweet and Miss Wynn scream at each other the day before—that was, before she remembered herself and hastened to intervene. It was a good thing the whole incident had taken place while Louisa-Margaretta was speaking to Miss Byrd. Otherwise, there would have been a spectator there to encourage the two ladies.

Not long after, Louisa-Margaretta insisted on buying Judith a fine gown, and Judith felt every single minute of that time as a pinprick on her conscience. Each minute wasted on a trifling gown was a minute she was not spending looking for Morgan or convincing someone else to look for him.

Louisa-Margaretta's argument was that the opera was their best chance with the Beefsteak Club members, and as soon as they had more personal connections with those in power, they could argue about Morgan's safe return.

"Mr Beecham is quite taken with you, Judith," she said, tracing a particularly lovely bolt of satin as Mrs Norman, deferential thanks to the impressive wealth of Louisa-Margaretta's parents, looked on. "Continue to flatter him, and he may be foolish enough to go to France himself."

"You oughtn't joke about things like that," said Judith, her heart leaping into her throat. "I have never sought Mr Beecham's attention, and I'm quite sure no young man shall be getting on a boat to France if they have no intention of fighting."

Louisa-Margaretta shook her head. "And what are you going to do? Stow away on a military vessel? We have to convince at least one of them, and Mr Beecham is the easiest mark."

These words were still ringing in Judith's head the next day. When she and Louisa-Margaretta were in the music room, looking through the score of Mr Solier's opera and Mr Coleman's notes on the revisions, Judith glared at her friend when Mr Beecham interrupted them.

Louisa-Margaretta, of course, seemed quite pleased.

"Dear Mr Beecham," she said. "What? No Mr Cartwright or Mr Hartsock? I was beginning to think the three of you were never apart."

"*Au contraire*, Miss Haddington," he said, settling comfortably in an old, rather threadbare chair next to the little table where the ladies were working. "Cartwright stays out far too late to rise this early, and Hartsock had some sort of obligation to his wife, though he would have liked to join me."

"Such trouble, when one is legally shackled to the whims of a lady," said Louisa-Margaretta. "Even when the lady is the lovely Susannah."

Judith pursed her lips at her friend's rudeness.

But Mr Beecham either didn't notice or pretended perfect sincerity. "Yes, well, Hartsock does complain a great deal. But at any rate, I'm thankful to have this opportunity to join you at the theatre. What did you wish to speak to me about?"

Judith fumed. It was most clear that Louisa-Margaretta had been behind the little meeting, and she resolved to escape Mr Beecham as soon as politeness would allow.

"I think all is well," said Judith.

"Because all ends well?" ventured Mr Beecham. "Mind you, I was never much good with the Bard's work in school."

"It is no matter," said Louisa-Margaretta. "And all is not well, Judith. This production shall go bankrupt without a rescuer now Mr Fortescue is dead."

Judith touched her friend's hand. "But that is not our business to share with the world, is it?"

Louisa-Margaretta glared. "For shame, Judith! I would have hoped you might wish prosperity on your cousin Jasper. What will become of his prospects if he doesn't get to perform his very excellent role?"

"He shall find another," murmured Judith, but Mr Beecham was already interested.

"Indeed, I'd no idea! And you say that Mr Fortescue was going to help the theatre? That is passing extraordinary. I know the Byrds had sought his patronage in the past, but I'm afraid he always laughed at the notion."

Judith looked closely at Louisa-Margaretta, but she needn't have worried. If her friend excelled in any area, it was inventing stories—or, as some would say, lies—when necessary.

"Well, he saw the error of his ways," said Louisa-Margaretta. "He was prepared to pay for many weeks of the run, but then, we all know how rich he was! I'm sure no more than a few days of costs would see them through. That is, if you can manage such a contribution, Mr Beecham."

"Oh," said the man, taken aback for a moment, and Judith wondered if her friend had misperceived his finances. "Well, perhaps I could ask Hartsock—"

"Your friends are, of course, welcome to contribute," said Louisa-Margaretta. And before Mr Beecham could say no to her, she rushed out of the room. "I'll just go find Miss Byrd and tell her the news!"

Judith sighed. "I must apologise for my friend, Mr Beecham."

The gentleman smiled, sighed, and gave a low chuckle. As he did so, he leaned closer to her. "No apologies necessary, Miss St Clair. Little Miss Haddington was always quite a spitfire when we were children, and I'm pleased to see she has lost none of her spirit. If anything, she has gained more over the years."

Judith considered his statement. Their trip to Russia had, for Louisa-Margaretta, been a low point. But when she returned to English shores, French fiancé in tow, her character had seemed to take on its stubborn, confident contours once again. It was a relief for Judith, who had hated to see her dear friend out of spirits for an entire winter, but it also presented certain problems, one of them being the fact that Mr Beecham was looking beseechingly at her, clearly thankful for the time alone in the little room. Since the door was open, Judith wasn't scared of Mr Beecham attempting any impropriety, but she wondered whether he was quite clear on the finer points of her engagement.

Instead of speaking of it, though, in her embarrassment, Judith grabbed the scores.

"We are fortunate," she said, trying to keep her face from flushing. "Mr Coleman had very little to say about Mr Solier's opera. Miss Byrd visited him yesterday with some of the actresses, and he's going to allow it to go forward with only minor revisions."

"What is the title?" asked Mr Beecham.

"*La exilée*," said Judith.

"Exile, is that right? I was never much good at French, though eventually, I realized that one is laughed out of the best circles without some command of the language."

Judith's French was excellent, as she had worked hard at her studies, and she never much liked it when lazy members of Louisa-Margaretta's circles claimed they were not "good at French" because of their lack of effort. Even Louisa-Margaretta, who had always neglected her studies, spoke quite passable French after spending months with Mr Solier.

But she was not going to say as much to Mr Beecham. All she needed to do, Judith reminded herself, was make polite conversation until Miss Byrd came through the door. Though she did wonder how Louisa-Margaretta had failed to find the director already. One would think she could not be far.

"It's a female exile," Judith explained. "The opera is about a woman."

Mr Beecham nodded. "But drawing on the man's own experience, I'm sure. It was clever to disguise it."

Judith paused for a moment. Perhaps Mr Beecham was more insightful than she'd first imagined.

"It is very brave," she agreed. "Mr Solier is speaking of his experience, which has been very hard indeed, but in a comedic context. The exploits of Marie are so ridiculous that few would think to compare her with the composer."

They were silent, and Mr Beecham shifted in his seat.

"I understand you and Louisa-Margaretta have been through some considerable adventures yourselves," he said. "To think most English ladies do not even attempt a Grand Tour, yet you've been in the emperor's palace in St Petersburg!"

Judith gave a bland smile. If Mr Beecham had known what actually happened in the Winter Palace, he would not be speaking of it with such reverence. Then again, perhaps he disapproved of their visiting at all. From his tone, she couldn't be sure.

"Do you think it's better for an English lady to remain always on English shores, Mr Beecham?" she asked, trying to make it clear that no answer he gave would offend her while also pondering ways she might make him leave.

"No, of course not. Only I cannot help thinking you are both rather better suited for lives in politics than other young ladies might be. You speak other languages, you are not afraid of travel, and you are quite comfortable in spaces such as this one."

He gestured with his arm, indicating the music room, with its shabby furniture and uneven decor.

Judith, unable to keep silent any longer, explained her situation.

"My fiancé, Mr Ramsbury, has begun a career as a diplomat," she said quickly. "And I should hope that not only my travels but my upbringing as well have prepared me to be a suitable wife for a man in such a position."

She did not say that she was, in fact, well-suited in her

own right to understand and solve international disputes—even, in fact, search for murderers, just as Mr Fudge was attempting to do at present. But before Mr Beecham could respond, Judith continued spelling out her plight. After all, if Louisa-Margaretta could ask Mr Beecham for a great deal of money, she might as well plead her own case.

"Mr Ramsbury is one of the men who has been missing since the Congress of Vienna," said Judith. "Nobody knows what happened to his party. But with so many of our young men being sent to France now, if a few of them could be dispatched to discover them, what a relief it would bring to the family! Especially to Miss Haddington and her parents."

"Oh," said Mr Beecham. But before he could finish his thought, they were interrupted by the Duke of Ormonde, who wandered into the room with a wide smile.

"Well, hello there! Have you seen Miss Sweet, by any chance? Or Miss Wynn?"

When he asked for the second actress, his voice was lower, and Judith tried to keep herself from frowning. The Duke of Ormonde seemed so kind and deferential yet so brazen in his affections. Each time she saw the man, her opinion of him grew worse. It would be one thing if he had simply transferred his attentions from Miss Wynn to Miss Sweet. That would have been dishonourable enough, but to continue to pay court to the first while bestowing favours upon the second was quite another.

Mr Beecham was plainly not as shocked as Judith. His smile was a bit strained, but he nodded. "I saw Miss Sweet in the green room. As far as I'm aware, Miss Wynn is still on the stage, practicing one of her scenes with Mr St Clair."

The duke smirked. "Excellent, excellent. Thank you, sir."

He walked on, and Judith tried to avert her eyes. She did not wish to see whom the duke would favor. In fact, the whole incident felt so very distasteful to her that she felt like leaving the theatre entirely, but she would need to stay in case Miss Byrd had questions about the revisions. Louisa-Margaretta would be happy to answer such queries, of course, but since she had done very little of the work, her answers might well be wrong.

Mr Beecham had still not answered her inquiry about Morgan, but Judith felt too embarrassed to press him. He had probably not realised she was engaged, and if she gave him an opportunity, he might make excuses as to why sending soldiers to find Morgan was not practical. And she could not let that happen.

"Let us go and find my cousin," she said, standing briskly. "I have a few things to ask about his role in *La exilée* before I put down all the changes."

Mr Beecham stood and followed Judith, on familiar ground again now that they were speaking of the theatre.

"Will Mr St Clair be pleased with the part, do you think?"

Judith gave a strained smile. "Well, as an actor, he might say it is not his place to be pleased or displeased with it. But they all have their opinions, of course. I imagine he will like the music, though I can hardly think how we will make the revisions stick. Mr Solier's creation is rather perfect as it is, and I'm not at all sure my French is quite up to the task. It is one thing to have a conversation but quite another to make sure a libretto is poetical enough."

"Why not ask the man himself to do it?"

Judith shook her head emphatically. "He would refuse. Already, he has compared this opera to a living child! No, even the revisions I do make will be hateful to him, but he must live with them if he wishes to see this performed in London."

Mr Beecham laughed in agreement, and Judith felt herself smiling just for a moment. Truly, Mr Beecham was very pleasant company.

If only she had not asked him for such a very great favor. Perhaps he would begin to avoid her.

30

———

Louisa-Margaretta was coming away from the green room when she saw Judith and Mr Beecham in the passage. Their little conversation must have gone even better than she'd hoped, though Judith would not have done anything improper. Her cousin Morgan was perfectly safe. His future wife would never betray him.

Louisa-Margaretta, on the other hand, was all too easily swayed by passion. So many times, she'd wished she could be like Judith... kind but cool-headed enough to put anyone off. How many grave mistakes Louisa-Margaretta could have avoided. But she knew it to be perfectly impossible. She was just as hot-blooded as the actresses, though she did not envy them a life of having to memorise odd little rhymes and strut about onstage.

"Judith, Mr Beecham, how fortunate," she said. "Mr Beecham, Miss Byrd is in the audience, working on where the actors are going to stand during the rehearsal. She begs you to come to her, as she would like to discuss the financial arrangements. Meanwhile, she had some particular request for Mr St Clair, and I have been sent to find him."

"Excellent," said Mr Beecham, though he was clearly sorry to leave Judith. "I will find her now. Miss Haddington, Miss St Clair, I hope you have a lovely morning."

"I wish you the same, Mr Beecham," said Louisa-Margaretta, whereas Judith managed only a vague "Yes" said to the back of the departing man.

As soon as he was out of hearing, Louisa-Margaretta grinned at her friend.

"So, what do you think? Is he in love with you?"

Judith winced. "Don't tease me, Louisa-Margaretta. I don't deserve it."

"Ah, but he will be quite interested in paying for the production now. I knew he would be susceptible to a pretty face."

Judith frowned. "My face is plain, Louisa-Margaretta. Somehow, it is only around you that I seem to meet with this sort of attention."

Louisa-Margaretta smiled, patting Judith's head as if she were a child.

"This is because you don't understand how things work in the *haut ton*, Judith. It is not fashionable to have opinions, be intelligent, or not care about money and prestige in marriage. When men meet a woman like you, they are entranced with her, particularly if she has pleasing features. Which you do, though they do not quite follow all the standard conventions of beauty. Much like my father's features, in fact, and enough ladies seemed to favor him."

Judith smiled again. "That is probably because of his wealth, is it not?"

"Very true," agreed Louisa-Margaretta. "Money is a great help. It would have helped Mr Fortescue find a bride, were he not such a horrid monster."

Judith winced. "Louisa-Margaretta, for heaven's sake,

lower your voice. We cannot be heard saying such things about him."

"You know me, Judith," said Louisa-Margaretta even more loudly. "I've never believed that one cannot speak ill of the dead. Especially when, as in the case of Mr Fortescue, there is nothing good that could possibly be said."

Judith looked about them. Louisa-Margaretta had knocked on the door of each dressing room, but she had received not one response.

"They all ought to be onstage," Louisa-Margaretta murmured. "Yet your cousin eludes us."

They did not have to look far, as Jasper came striding over at that moment, his face flushed.

"Judith, Miss Haddington," he said. "How fortunate! You have come to help with these revisions, I assume."

"We haven't finished the ones for the comic opera yet," said Judith. "But Mr Coleman approved everything else, so the show ought to be able to go forward."

Jasper gave a little laugh. "Yes, well, we've got to remember all of the new ones. But Miss Byrd is determined that we shall open the day after tomorrow, with no further delays, and she tends to get her way."

"Interesting that her father cannot check her," said Louisa-Margaretta. "Surely, as owner and controller of the purse, he ought to be able to decide. That was certainly my impression the other day."

She did not appreciate Judith's amused smile.

"Tell me, dear Louisa-Margaretta," Judith said. "Has your father ever been able to keep you from doing exactly as you wished?"

Jasper said quietly, "The rumors all have it that Mr Byrd bought this theatre for his daughter."

Louisa-Margaretta blinked. "Well, she is an expert, then!

My father has never bought me something half so nice as an opera house. Whatever was the reason?"

When Jasper didn't answer, Judith gave him a sympathetic smile. "You needn't tell us. It's none of our business, at any rate."

"No," said Jasper. "But it is probably evident enough from what you've seen so far."

Louisa-Margaretta had no idea what he meant, but that did not stop her from encouraging him. "Yes, of course, dear Mr St Clair. So there can be no harm in telling us."

"Louisa-Margaretta," moaned Judith.

But Jasper only leaned in. "Miss Byrd is not happy being idle. She did not wish to marry, and her father was afraid that without an occupation she would be... unwell."

"Mad, you mean," said Louisa-Margaretta. "My dear cousin, it is no secret in the family that dear Judith and I have spent a good deal of time in a madhouse."

"It's not a—"

"Hush, Judith. That's exactly what it is, only I agree with you that it's a rather nice one. So you need not hesitate to use such words in front of us, Mr St Clair. I can assure you we have none of the usual ladylike delicacy around this subject."

"I... I was not aware, no, not exactly. But then, of course, you will understand Miss Byrd's position and her father's."

"We do," said Judith, shooting Louisa-Margaretta a reproachful look. "Louisa-Margaretta, I believe you had a message for my cousin."

"Yes. You are to go see Miss Byrd about the hat you're wearing in the first act. Though why she doesn't leave that to the wardrobe mistress, I can't imagine."

"Thank you," said Jasper. "I shall do so now."

After he walked off, Louisa-Margaretta frowned. "Judith,

you'll have to be the one to find out why your cousin is lying."

Judith looked away. "Louisa-Margaretta, I do not suspect my cousin of this terrible crime," she said. "And if he is not always truthful, well, let he who is without sin, et cetera."

Louisa-Margaretta laughed. "You can leave off quoting scripture at me, Judith. I hear enough of that from my mother. Although it's been some time since she's done more than put it all in a letter."

"Do you miss her?" asked Judith. "I'll confess that I do, even if she still despises me."

Louisa-Margaretta waved her hand. "That was all long ago, Judith, and if she has not forgiven you for my unhappy return from that madhouse, she is a fool."

Judith sighed. "She is not a fool. We could write to hasten her arrival in London, you know, although I imagine she has already left with your father—"

"Judith," said Louisa-Margaretta. "You are trying to distract me, and while it may work for a moment, the fact remains that your cousin is hiding something. This is not even a large theatre, yet one can never find him when he is needed. He stays out half the time. He is very secretive—"

"He and Dorothy are not well-suited. You have seen for yourself that she hates the life he has chosen, though she despises being under her parents' thumb even more. What the woman needs is her own home."

"Then she ought to buy one," said Louisa-Margaretta stoutly.

Judith only sighed, no doubt thinking of her cousin's paltry meals and weak tea. Even to Louisa-Margaretta, it was clear that Dorothy St Clair could not afford to purchase a home. But if she were clever, like Miss Byrd, she would convince someone to buy one for her.

"Let's go fix your fiancé's work," she said with a glimmer of enthusiasm. Hard work always animated Judith, though Louisa-Margaretta felt just the opposite.

"Very well," she said. "If we must. I suppose the show must go on."

But as they started in on Mr Coleman's meticulous corrections, Louisa-Margaretta noticed that her friend was distracted. And that only confirmed for her what she had been thinking all morning.

Something was seriously wrong with Mr Jasper St Clair. And Judith, deny it all she liked, was aware of the fact.

31

———

That afternoon, Jasper burst into the little rented rooms, a haunted look in his eyes.

"How was the rehearsal?" asked Dorothy.

But Jasper ignored her. "It's that Fudge again."

Annoyance passed over Dorothy's face, but Louisa-Margaretta seemed pleased to hear the news.

"What has our magistrate been doing?" she asked. "Do you need me to use my influence with him?"

Judith gave Louisa-Margaretta a sharp look. Though her friend had been coy as to the particulars, it seemed clear that Mr Fudge had paid her some rather pointed attention in the past. Whatever the outcome, Judith was clear that Louisa-Margaretta had surely not encouraged such actions. She and Mr Fudge would have been wildly different in terms of both age and temperament, and all the instances she had known in which a stepmother was hardly older than her stepchildren had ended in tension and misunderstandings.

"It wouldn't do any good," said Jasper. "He always gets vexed when he's unable to find a culprit, or so they tell me.

And anyone in the theatre could have poisoned Mr Fortescue. He just likes me the best for it."

"But he hasn't arrested you," said Judith. Her heart was fluttering, but she had helped others through such circumstances and hoped to do the same for her cousin. She went to him, showing him to a chair.

"If he believed so strongly in your guilt, Jasper, he would have locked you up," said Judith, trying to keep your voice steady.

"Oh heavens, what is to become of me if you are in prison?" wailed Dorothy.

Louisa-Margaretta shot the latter a dark look. "No hysterics. Nobody is going to prison. Judith is right. Mr Fudge would not hesitate to act if he were sure of himself. You are home, and that means he is unsure."

"It doesn't matter," said Jasper. "How can this opera go forward if half the cast is suspected of murder? And how shall I ever land another role? Nobody is going to want me if they think I'll go about putting arsenic in the patrons' wine."

"Was it arsenic?" asked Louisa-Margaretta.

Jasper slouched in his chair. "I have no idea because I'm innocent."

Judith sighed. "We'll find a way to prove it."

He put his head in his hands. "I couldn't ask that of you. And there's no way you could do it even if I did."

"You could tell us everything you know about the cast members," said Louisa-Margaretta sharply. "Then we can decide for ourselves who is most suspicious and turn Mr Fudge's attention to that individual."

"Not if they're innocent," Judith broke in. "Besides, we already know a great deal about the cast and about Mr Fortescue."

"But you don't know what happened today," said Jasper.

"When we were there at the theatre?" asked Judith, confused.

"After you left. Mr Byrd was poisoned."

32

———

The call was Judith's idea.

"If we cannot convince Mr Fudge to leave my cousin alone, the least we can do is tell him the other things we've noticed in the theatre," she told Louisa-Margaretta.

"Mr Fudge will hardly be interested in our opinions. He is a man and a proud one. If we can get him a message anonymously, identifying the killer but allowing him to take credit, that is the only thing that will sway him."

Judith gave Louisa-Margaretta a curious look. Many years ago, when Mr Fudge had unjustly connected Jasper to the disappearance of a young lady, similar tactics had been called for. But Judith had thought she was alone in her understanding of Mr Fudge's character. Though he was honest, he was proud, and he might not be able to accept a solution if it came directly from a lady. Louisa-Margaretta, though she was chiefly concerned with herself, could be surprisingly perceptive at times.

"Be that as it may," said Judith, "we have had a very easy time getting about the theatre. We have gone in and out of all sorts of rooms, borrowed items, and found parts of costumes. The fact is anyone could have put poison in Mr Fortescue's wine. Perhaps poison that was not even meant for that gentleman. And now that Mr Byrd is suffering, it is plain that anyone at all might be responsible."

Louisa-Margaretta shrugged. "Judith, we have saved this opera by fixing everything Mr Coleman disliked, flirting with Mr Beecham to secure the funding, and soothing the feelings of all these temperamental actors." Though Judith furrowed her brow at the mention of Mr Beecham, she continued. "But the fact remains that we still haven't the slightest idea who committed the murder. Admit it. We have almost nothing to go on."

Judith straightened her hat. "I shall admit nothing of the sort. I am very confident that my cousin is innocent, and that is all I need to know."

"Oh, do you truly think so?" asked Dorothy, bursting out of her bedroom.

With a sour expression, Louisa-Margaretta said, "Dear Dorothy, there is no need to join us. Judith and I have the matter well in hand."

Dorothy blinked at them like a disappointed calf. "I had hoped to call on the family again. Young Miss Russ was ever so sweet."

At that, Judith blinked in surprise, and Louisa-Margaretta began to laugh. At least they knew the surname of the young woman who had referred to herself only as "Jenny."

"Sweet, you call it," said Louisa-Margaretta. "Clever, to be sure, and honest to a fault. But I'm sure that young girl has never been called sweet in her life."

"There is some quality to her," said Judith. "I'm not sure if I would call it sweet, but she was the only person in the family who understood Morgan's perilous situation. Even at her young age, she grasped it better than the rest of them."

"Well, we must hope she grasps the facts of this murder better than her uncle Christmas," said Louisa-Margaretta. "Come along, then, Dorothy. I'm sure it won't hurt your brother to have one more defender."

33

———

The call was so early as to be considered rather rude, but Judith knew they could not risk visiting without being admitted to see Mr Fudge.

And indeed, since they arrived early, they saw almost the whole family. Mrs Stone and Miss Russ were awake, as was Mr Christmas Fudge, though apparently, young Mr Felton Fudge and his sister were still sleeping.

"This is an unexpected pleasure," said the elder Mr Fudge.

"Well, I'm afraid it is not purely a social call," said Judith gently. "We are very concerned about the accusations against my cousin, and we hoped to share all we know about the Lyceum Theatre to help you find the responsible party."

"I see," said Mr Christmas Fudge. He had a knack for giving inscrutable responses that were usually particular to ladies of the *haut ton*, but Judith was fairly sure that those involved with the law ended up with similar tendencies.

"What's your cousin accused of?" asked Mrs Stone.

"The families always think one of their own didn't do it,"

said Miss Russ. "But the person who did it, mark my words, is family to someone."

Her grandmother bristled. "We needn't speak to Miss St Clair in those terms, I'm sure."

Judith tried to hide a smile. "I'm well aware that every person on earth has family members—at least, those of us who are blessed to know our families," she said. "We only wanted to make sure Mr Christmas Fudge had all the facts."

"What are those, then?" asked Miss Russ with greater interest.

Louisa-Margaretta turned to Dorothy. "You know more about that theatre than anyone," she said. "Tell Mr Fudge a bit about what goes on there."

Dorothy, for all she had begged to come, sat without saying a word. She looked as if she were about to cry. Judith's heart went out to the young woman.

Louisa-Margaretta had faced a similar ordeal when one of her own brothers was imprisoned for a murder he did not commit. But she spared no sympathy for Dorothy. "Look alive, dear Miss St Clair. For we have such welcoming hosts!"

Neither Mrs Stone nor Miss Russ, who was sitting darkly on the settee, casting glances at her abandoned novel all the while, looked particularly welcoming.

"Well," said Judith, feeling uneasy, "we have discovered a few things about the Lyceum Theatre. First, that it is not particularly difficult to gain admittance and that other groups use the facilities for their own gatherings."

"Though they were not doing so at the time the incident took place," said Mr Christmas Fudge.

"Yes," said Louisa-Margaretta. "But the place is akin to a cathedral or a very large museum. Who knows what sort of person may be going out? And wine, of which Mr Fortescue was rather overfond, can be poisoned at any moment."

The grandmother frowned, and Judith hastily took over from her friend. "What Miss Haddington means to say, I think, is that my cousin had no reason at all to harm Mr Fortescue."

"Is there anything else that you can tell us?" asked Mr Fudge. "I must ask you ladies to pardon me, but I'm sure you will have heard what happened with Mr Byrd. I am really rather busy."

Dorothy took out her handkerchief and began dabbing at her eyes. At that very moment, Mr Felton Fudge came in. He looked quite awake, but he had plainly made a mess of his toilette, as his necktie was askew and his hair rather disheveled. Judith wondered why he had not called one of the Fudge family's many servants to help him.

"Papa, what have you done?" he asked, glaring at his father before striding over to Dorothy with a handkerchief. "My dear Miss St Clair, I am so sorry."

Judith turned her attention from Dorothy's sniffles to Mr Christmas Fudge's uneasy speculations.

"I can well believe that other people might have disliked Mr Fortescue," said Mr Christmas Fudge, and Louisa-Margaretta brightened.

"However," he continued sternly, "I don't believe for a moment that someone who was not at the theatre managed to poison him with a quick-acting substance."

"But it does not follow that the person who did so was my cousin," said Judith quietly. She heard the tremor in her voice and cursed herself for appearing weak in front of the man who held all the power over him.

"Of course not," he said. "But again, this is hardly a suitable discussion for a family circle. I have a reputation for fairness, Miss St Clair, and you can be assured that an innocent man will not be found guilty of this crime."

Louisa-Margaretta grimaced, but Judith shot her a warning look. Their dismissal was clear.

"Of course, Mr Fudge," said Judith, trying to sound sweet and unconcerned. "Your reputation precedes you."

She did not say that part of what she considered to be his reputation was his knack for pestering the innocent, especially people with few connections like Jasper. At least, to his credit, Mr Christmas Fudge did not allow the rich to get away with their crimes by rote. The entire system might favor the wealthy, but one could not call Mr Fudge corrupt.

"Ladies," said Judith, clearing her throat. "I believe we must be going."

Louisa-Margaretta gave a stiff nod, and Dorothy shot Judith a look that was nothing short of murderous, but there was nothing they could accomplish by staying. Mr Fudge had not been swayed from his conviction that Jasper, Mr Daw, or Mr Nightingale was guilty, and nothing they could say appeared to convince him otherwise.

The three ladies took their leave, but Louisa-Margaretta paused as soon as they had been decorously shown out of the elegant residence.

"One moment," said Louisa-Margaretta. "I wanted to say one last thing to Miss Russ. Wait for me outside, Judith."

Judith stood on the pavement with Dorothy, wilting in the heat.

"Your friend will be speaking with one of those men," she said. "Mark my words."

Judith sighed. "She's an engaged woman, Dorothy."

"Yes, engaged to a man we seldom see."

"There is no reason to think she will not be faithful to Mr Solier," said Judith faintly, though in fact, there were plenty of reasons to think so. Louisa-Margaretta was not a young woman who could tolerate a marriage devoid of true passion and devotion. But when the engagement began, Louisa-Margaretta had considered it her very best option, and nothing that had happened since had convinced her otherwise.

"Are you both ready to go?" asked Louisa-Margaretta. "Mr Fudge didn't appreciate our visit, I daresay, so we really shouldn't spend another moment here."

"We've been waiting for you," grumbled Dorothy, and with that, they began the long, hot walk back to the St Clair residence.

34

Louisa-Margaretta met Jasper and Miss Byrd at the theatre. Judith would not approve, and though she was not certain about Miss Byrd's character, she did know that the latter would stop at nothing when it came to protecting the run of the opera. Perhaps she had even poisoned her own father.

Although in fact, the poison had not caused his death. When Louisa-Margaretta asked after him, Miss Byrd responded, her voice tight with anger or some other emotion, "He is recovering at home. The doctor says he will yet be well."

"That is excellent news," said Louisa-Margaretta.

"Not if we never find the culprit," said Miss Byrd. "I'm not sure how much I will be able to help you, Miss Haddington, but I must try."

"You must, indeed." Louisa-Margaretta noted that Miss Byrd seemed harried but determined.

And in spite of her poor acting, she looked rather well as a young gentleman.

"They'll know from my voice that I'm not a gentleman at all," fretted Miss Byrd.

Jasper grinned. "Then you had best not speak. Isn't that correct, Louisa-Margaretta?"

He had always called her Miss Haddington, but his disguise had made him bold. He was also quickly trading his accent for one that was a bit gruffer, not so poor that his fine hands would give him away but not as elegant as that of a gently brought up boy either.

"You may sit and drink your beer, Miss Byrd," said Louisa-Margaretta. "Look happy or sad as the occasion requires, and the others in the tavern will all try to fill the silence."

Jasper looked at himself in the long mirror. "Do I look convincing, then?"

Louisa-Margaretta nodded. "Yes. You work hard, but you're a bit of a dandy. What is it you do, then?"

"I was in the Navy. I'm about to join up again, go give that Napoleon Bonaparte a taste of his own medicine. Only I've stopped in London first to see a lady."

Miss Byrd rolled her eyes. "Yes, yes, very well."

"What is your own story, young sir?" Louisa-Margaretta asked Miss Byrd. In addition to her usual trousers, she was wearing a shirt and jacket along with a very well-done wig that was mostly covered by a cap.

"I'm not speaking," said Miss Byrd, shuddering.

"There's the spirit," said Louisa-Margaretta. "Have a lovely time!"

Jasper waited for her to go into the green room before he left with Miss Byrd. Louisa-Margaretta wished she could have joined them, but her face looked indelibly feminine no matter how she might try to disguise it. The sort of haunt Jasper and Miss Byrd were visiting was no place for a young woman, so she would have to be content with her supporting role in the plan.

Waiting in the theatre for their return, Louisa-Margaretta. Miss Byrd had insisted that the Daws stay with her, presumably so she was not murdered, but that forced her to sit in the green room with a remarkably dull novel and listen to the two of them reminisce about their early days in the theatre.

"Kill Claudio," said Mr Daw. "Ah, 'Kill Claudio!' That was your most glorious line, Sarah! I've never forgotten your delivery. And to think I was cast as Claudio! It hurt my feelings, that did."

Mrs Daw smiled more broadly than Louisa-Margaretta had ever seen.

"Both those men deserved to die," she said, "Benedick and Claudio. I've never liked that story. Why end with a wedding for people who don't deserve it?"

"The redemptive power of love, my dear," said Mr Daw with such seriousness that Louisa-Margaretta was sure he must be joking.

"Nonsense," said Mrs Daw. "And all that about Hero needing to be a maid. I'm sure that was out of date when the Bard wrote it, and it's certainly even worse now."

"Well, we shall never stop seeing it performed, my dear."

"It's enough that I can stop performing in it myself. Though I must admit our Angel and dear Theodosia would be lovely heroines in that one, wouldn't they?"

"They would," Mr Daw agreed. "Though not as lovely as you were."

"Stop it," said Mrs Daw.

Louisa-Margaretta thought she might be sick. It was rather indecent, the way some married couples kept flirting with each other well into old age. Her parents seemed to still have some genuine affection for each other, but if they engaged in such banter, they certainly did not allow others to see it. Louisa-Margaretta's father hardly spoke, even when his children were about. He preferred to sit silently at the center of a merry crowd, smiling and only occasionally voicing his thoughts.

When Jasper and Miss Byrd finally entered, they were out of breath, but Miss Byrd looked jubilant.

"I didn't say a word," she said. "And you were quite right, Miss Haddington. The lads seemed to like it. Started calling me 'Slim' and buying me more drinks."

"And what did you discover?" asked Mr Daw. "I'm sure Mr Fortescue had his share of enemies, but I hope those young men were able to share more specifics."

"Well," said Jasper breathlessly, "he no longer has as many enemies in the form of young ladies and their mothers."

Louisa-Margaretta sat absolutely still. That was the one area of gossip she hoped the men of the tavern would not cover, but it appeared her hopes were in vain.

"He used to make a sort of sport of chasing the young women who took his fancy," continued Jasper. "But some time ago, he gave all that up."

"Any idea as to why?" asked Mrs Daw.

"Well, some people say that he must have fallen in love with one woman in particular. Taken a mistress, perhaps. But nobody is sure as to the lady's identity, and it seems unlikely that he would have been able to keep it such a well-guarded secret. So perhaps that is just a rumour after all."

"What else did people say?" said Louisa-Margaretta. "Did he have debts?"

Miss Byrd shook her head. "The opposite. He liked

having others in his debt. Money, for him, was power, and he never hesitated to use it."

"Anyone in particular?" asked Mrs Daw.

"No, not that we could find," said Jasper. "He was beloved by most of the tradesmen, as he never took advantage of credit. Instead, he would pay them then have some penniless gentleman be in debt to him directly. He was always settling others' bills for this reason."

Louisa-Margaretta was shocked. "When they could have easily bought these things on credit, why would they turn to him?"

Mr Daw gave a smile. "Many of the sellers do not like this practise of offering credit to all gentlemen, Miss Haddington. They struggle with it, especially when they're unable to pursue these men for their debts."

Louisa-Margaretta blinked. Without credit, she would have been able to purchase nothing in London, not even that relatively modest gown she'd bought Judith the other day. At least she knew her father was good for it.

Mrs Daw was thoughtful. "But what of specifics, then? Is there one person who was widely considered to be his enemy?"

Jasper shook his head. "He criticized everyone. Quakers, Catholics, French emigres, poets. But he was always careful to explain that it was all simply a joke, so one couldn't punish him harshly for any of his views."

Louisa-Margaretta despised men who always claimed to be joking. It didn't surprise her that Mr Fortescue had been slippery.

"How did he make his fortune?" she asked. She now knew from experience that in cases of murder, money was often the root cause.

Miss Byrd sat up straighter. "Indeed, Miss Haddington,

that is an interesting story! He inherited most of it, but they did speak of some investments that have become remarkably profitable."

"Tell us," said Mr Daw. He and his wife looked quite interested, and though they were both excellent actors, Louisa-Margaretta was sure that none of their enthusiasm was feigned.

"The war," said Jasper. "If the man has anything of a genius about him, it's this. He knew that the Congress of Vienna was not going to end all the wars, and he invested accordingly."

Louisa-Margaretta looked away. Judith would hate to hear such a thing said aloud, but it made perfect sense to her. Even without Napoleon Bonaparte, one could hardly credit the idea of a lasting peace among habitually warring nations. With the return of the Corsican devil, it seemed quite impossible.

"He must have been doing well from his investments," said Mrs Daw. "Who will inherit his fortune?"

Jasper leaned in. "Everyone is asking. The rumor is that they haven't been able to locate a single blood relation apart from that friend of his in the Beefsteak Club. On the Asiatic side of his family, it is impossible to know, and on the English side, his origins are rather murky, though that cousin is somehow connected by marriage."

"And there were no children?" asked Mrs Daw quietly. Illegitimate children, she meant, and Louisa-Margaretta saw that the entire room understood.

"Well, that is a most relevant question," said Louisa-Margaretta before the conversation could take another turn. She didn't want someone to bring up Mr Fortescue's affections again as they speculated on whether he had fathered a child. "But we aren't likely to get the answer tonight. Mr St

Clair, Miss Byrd, very well done. We can take all this information to the magistrate in due course."

Jasper's face lost its animation, and at once, he looked very tired.

"Mr Christmas Fudge? You can't expect anything more from that man."

"I can expect that he shall make the right decision and keep you out of jail," said Louisa-Margaretta crisply, though she wondered. Jasper St Clair did not seem to be a killer to her. Yet she would hardly have blamed him if he had murdered Mr Fortescue. She just couldn't think of a single reason for him to do it.

Though she was quite determined to find out what he was hiding.

"Come, Mr St Clair," she said. "You must rest before the performance tomorrow."

"Will you be in attendance when the gentlemen leave the funeral, Miss Haddington?" asked Mrs Daw.

Louisa-Margaretta gave the woman an uneasy glance. The small figure, who had once seemed rather meek and maternal, had a mind that was much sharper than Louisa-Margaretta had initially guessed.

"I'm not sure if I have a suitable gown," she said.

"Mr Daw and I will be attending to pay our respects. Not the funeral or the burial, mind, but we will be sure to be in sight of the procession."

Louisa-Margaretta stared for a moment. "Oh. Thank you, Mrs Daw. I may very well do the same."

35

———

Judith was still awake when Louisa-Margaretta came in.

"Where have you been?" she asked. "Dorothy said you were at the theatre, but they were done rehearsing ages ago."

Judith had not undressed, though she felt very weary. She had an ancient shawl draped about her shoulders and a Bible next to her.

Louisa-Margaretta sighed. "Judith, your trouble is that you are quite pretty, but you never care about looking well. We ought to get you something more becoming than this old shawl."

"It is warm, and it was my mother's," said Judith.

"I'm sorry," said Louisa-Margaretta, words she almost never uttered.

Judith gave a weary smile. "I don't keep it simply because it was hers. But I like that it has lasted for decades. And if it gets a hole or two, they're easy enough to mend."

Louisa-Margaretta sat down next to Judith. "Silk would suit you better," she said firmly. "To answer your question, I have been to the theatre, but dear Jasper and Miss Byrd have been to a tavern!"

Jasper, who was entering the home at just that moment, took off his hat.

"Good night, Judith," he said. "Rest well, Louisa-Margaretta."

After he had left the room, Louisa-Margaretta pouted.

"You needn't give me that look, Judith," she said. "I'm not going to become a St Clair. There is no risk of my throwing poor Mr Solier over. I've had rather enough scandal for one lifetime."

Judith's fingers were exploring the one hole in the shawl she had yet to mend.

"I'm sorry for making assumptions," she said. But the familiarity between her friend and her cousin concerned her.

"Let me tell you all they learned," said Louisa-Margaretta. She described the trip to the tavern as if she had actually gone herself, which Judith hoped very much she had not.

"So what is your conclusion?" asked Judith slowly. "It seems much as we thought—Mr Fortescue had a great deal of enemies."

Louisa-Margaretta's smile was far too bright for the lateness of the hour. "Oh, but I realised something. I could never say it quite so plainly in front of all that group. We have knowledge of Mr Fortescue that they don't share."

"Yes. We know what sort of manner of man Mr Fortescue was in private, and I should think we must keep that a secret."

"Of course," said Louisa-Margaretta hastily. "And now he is dead, that should be simple enough. But we may as well look for culprits where Mr Christmas Fudge shall fear to tread."

"In the theatre? That's where he's looking already."

"He is not considering the actresses. Or Miss Byrd, though I wonder about her trying to kill her own father. Perhaps she only gave him enough poison to frighten him, knowing he wouldn't die. Have you heard the news? Mr and Mrs Daw told me he is recovering but that he had quite a scare."

Judith shook her head. "Oh, how ghastly."

Louisa-Margaretta sighed. "I do not know if it was her or Miss Sweet or Miss Wynn. Or Mrs Daw, for that matter. When she was speaking of *Much Ado About Nothing*, she said that both Claudio and Benedick ought to be killed."

Judith smiled. It had been some time since she had read Shakespeare's works, but she and Miriam had both adored them at one time. It was one of the few points on which the two sisters agreed in terms of their taste in literature. Miriam loved the dramatic nature of the plays and Judith, the beautiful language.

"I don't know that I completely disagree," she said thoughtfully. "But, Louisa-Margaretta, they are just men in a play."

"Men that Mrs Daw would like to murder," said Louisa-Margaretta. "You saw how Mr Fortescue was with Miss Sweet and Miss Wynn. Neither of them liked him, though they were too clever to say it aloud."

Judith sighed. "Is there anything else they mentioned that you thought might explain his death?"

"Of course. All his investments! If this war is a fast one, they shall be for naught."

"Wars are never fast," said Judith. Though her life had not been long, she felt she had at least enough experience to state that with some certainty. "People always speculate that they will end quickly, but they never do. Mark my words. We will lose many poor young men fighting Napoleon Bonaparte."

Louisa-Margaretta fiddled with Judith's shawl. "Well, all right. But even if you are correct, Judith, Mr Fortescue might have wanted a guarantee. Perhaps he found a way of seeing to it that our forces were not effective."

In spite of the heat of the night, Judith felt chilly. Plots that involved manipulating the actions of kings and governments terrified her. Though she was well versed in politics and history, she did not like to think that assassins existed, much less that they might be at work very near her.

"If that's the case, we shouldn't touch this," she said shortly.

Smiling, Louisa-Margaretta replied, "We ought to hope it's the case. Though how it would possibly affect Mr Byrd, I have no idea."

"Poor man. Do you know anything else about what happened to him?"

Louisa-Margaretta shook her head. "Your cousin spoke to Miss Byrd, and he told me everything on our way home. Apparently, they still don't know how Mr Byrd was poisoned, and he is refusing to leave the house. He has told his daughter not to go forward with the opera at all."

"But will he stop her?"

Louisa-Margaretta giggled. "Well done, Judith. Now you understand how wayward daughters think."

"I am wayward enough myself. I have not been home in ages."

"You can go home after I marry Mr Solier," said Louisa-Margaretta. "I could use some good riding and hunting, and he will be happy enough as long as he is at the pianoforte."

It was just the sort of separate living arrangement that suited many married couples, but Judith could not help worrying that her friend was presenting it as an ideal from the very beginning.

"Perhaps you could take him out riding," she said.

Louisa-Margaretta scoffed. "He has no interest. And he would only slow me down. After months without a horse, I have no patience for poor riders, including you, Judith."

Thinking of Derbyshire, Judith sighed. "I cannot leave London until I find out where Morgan is. And in the meantime, we have to tell Mr Fudge everything we know of Mr Fortescue."

Louisa-Margaretta laughed. "This was the work of one evening, Judith. If the magistrate had any interest, he could have discovered all this already."

"Your Mr Fudge is the one interrogating Jasper," said Judith. "I cannot in good conscience keep any of this information from him."

Louisa-Margaretta sniffed. "Then you shall have to go alone. If it was a woman, I shall find her using my own methods. And if Mr Fortescue was killed because he is a saboteur, well, I hope the person responsible finds a way to inform Mr Fudge directly, for we certainly have little hope of finding them."

36

Louisa-Margaretta hated being burdened with Dorothy. But the latter insisted she knew where the Daw residence was but could not recall the address, so they were forced to go together.

"It must be odd, walking so much," said Dorothy pointedly. "I'm sure you're used to having a carriage at your disposal in London."

Louisa-Margaretta, with some difficulty, kept herself from shoving the little St Clair lady to the side. Growing up with only elder brothers, she often had the impulse to use her fists in order to make her point known. Judith, by contrast, had worried her whole life about setting a proper example for her younger siblings, and she would not have approved if Louisa-Margaretta had pushed her cousin away. Though Dorothy might well benefit from tumbling into the path of a fast-moving carriage.

"You forget that your cousin Judith and I have been living the country life for some time," said Louisa-Margaretta. "I am quite used to walking, though of course I miss riding a great deal."

"Of course," said Dorothy without even an attempt at politeness.

Louisa-Margaretta stopped in the street. "I might remind you Judith and I are attempting to rescue *your* brother. He is in a very troublesome situation with the magistrate, and should you choose not to help us, you may well regret your actions later."

"I am doing all I can to help," said Dorothy. "And please do not pretend you are doing this only to help Jasper."

Louisa-Margaretta sighed. "I am rather excellent at unraveling such puzzles. It is true. But if it were only a question of finding the person who killed Mr Fortescue, I am not sure I should feel such urgency."

Dorothy frowned. "The culprit ought to hang for this. He probably *will* hang for it unless we are much mistaken in the character of Mr Christmas Fudge."

Her words were spoken carefully, as if she were afraid of offending Louisa-Margaretta by implying anything negative about the magistrate.

"I'm not sure whoever murdered Mr Fortescue *ought* to hang for his or her actions," said Louisa-Margaretta. "For all I know, the individual deserves all sorts of rewards for ridding the world of such a horrid person."

At last, she had found a way to keep Dorothy quiet. The poor little shocked woman did not say another word until they had reached the modest house where the Daws resided.

Mrs Daw was sitting in the parlor with Miss Sweet when the visitors were announced. Both rose in surprise but seemed quite sincere in their greetings.

"Dear Miss St Clair," said Miss Sweet. "We see so much of your brother and so little of you."

Dorothy nodded. "I will be there on opening night. In

the cheapest seat I can find, of course. I always am, though Jasper has said he cannot begin to see me from the stage."

Mrs Daw got up to order tea for the visitors then seated herself again. "That is immaterial, Miss St Clair. One feels the presence of a loved one. Is not that so, Angel? Whether we can see each face, well, that hardly signifies."

Miss Sweet looked just as lovely as her name as she gave her innocent smile. "Of course. And we're working so hard onstage that we're not able to look over the crowd and pick out individual faces. But that does not mean your presence doesn't matter. Mrs Daw and I will be thrilled to see you."

"I'm sure we can get an adequate seat," said Louisa-Margaretta. "Well, you all know what a cloud has been hanging over the production. I had hoped to ask both you ladies about Mr Fortescue. He has been reviled by most everyone we have spoken to so far, but did he give either of you any particular offense?"

She knew that subterfuge would hardly work on experienced actresses, so she had decided to ask them directly. But they only looked at each other without answering. A young servant came in with the tea, and Mrs Daw busied herself serving her guests with Miss Sweet's assistance.

Dorothy, ever unhelpful, looked mournfully out the window. "It must be lovely to excel in a profession such as yours, Miss Sweet."

The young lady blinked. "Well, it is work," she said. "But work that I very much hope to continue."

Dorothy sighed. "I am not suited for the theatre at all, I'm afraid. I feel as if I am living my brother's life rather than my own."

Miss Sweet coloured and was at a loss for words, but Mrs Daw nodded.

"I'm afraid that is the case for most women," she said.

"One lives based on the whims of a father, a brother, or perhaps a husband. If Mr Daw had asked me to leave the stage after our marriage, I'm sure I should have felt much the same."

Miss Sweet smiled at that. "He never asked you, not even at first?"

Mrs Daw shook her head. "Not everyone considers acting a respectable profession, as you are well aware. But Mr Daw and I have always felt that one ought to bring respectability to the stage rather than leaving the stage in pursuit of respectability."

Louisa-Margaretta bit her tongue. They were wasting time on such frivolous talk, and she had still gotten next to nothing of note on Mr Fortescue.

"Mrs Daw, did you know Mr Fortescue well?" she asked.

Mrs Daw shook her head. "I do not have a great many friends, dear. There are young men and women we help train for the stage as well as a handful of dear companions from my youth. But when it comes to the fashionable set, I must say I have neither curiosity nor affection for those young people. I simply cannot relate to their way of being."

Dorothy nodded strongly. "I feel just the same. But without the stage and with few of my own friends here, things are rather different."

"Perhaps you could go back to living with your family," said Miss Sweet. "You are fortunate to have them."

But Dorothy only shook her head. "It is even more difficult there. I would like to marry, but with my parents, it is more an obligation than a wish. Last time I lived with them, they kept forcing old landowners to come and pay court to me. I could not bear it."

Mrs Daw smiled. "We know all about unsuitable gentlemen paying court, do we not, Angel? One only has to become practised in the correct ways of discouraging them. Being an actress, of course, helps a great deal."

Louisa-Margaretta was embarrassed to hear the veiled reference to Miss Sweet's paramour. But she pressed forward, knowing that such a bold declaration might shock Judith, but it should not be news to her.

"Well, then," she said. "Tell me about Mr Fortescue's attentions. Did he expect any favors in return for his patronage of the theatre?"

"He had no right to expect such a thing," said Miss Sweet, flushing for the first time.

Louisa-Margaretta was satisfied to see that young Angel Sweet's face could display anger. She had never actually seen the woman angry with anyone other than Miss Wynn, but the single mention of Mr Fortescue's pursuits changed her countenance completely.

"More tea, dear?" asked Mrs Daw. "Miss St Clair?"

"Yes, I would love some," said Dorothy. "I must say it is very good."

Louisa-Margaretta sighed again. Dorothy, who had to bargain most mightily for old potatoes, was not able to spend a great deal on tea leaves, and Louisa-Margaretta had been tolerating the sad state of household affairs ever since she began staying with the St Clairs. She was very glad for a return to the strong-tasting beverage she was accustomed to drinking, although Mrs Daw's china was not as fine as any of the sets in Wycliff Castle.

"Yes, thank you, Mrs Daw. I would love another cup of tea. Only, what is your impression of Mr Fortescue's expectations?"

"You needn't pry," said Miss Sweet stiffly.

But Mrs Daw poured more tea for Louisa-Margaretta and pursed her lips.

"I'm not quite sure how to describe it," she said. "Other places are tolerant of great abuses of power, to be sure. But the Lyceum Theatre is unique. There is a reason Mr Daw and I feel comfortable bringing the young people we help to their doors, particularly the young ladies."

She began cutting slices of cake. Dorothy snatched at one with undisguised greed. Louisa-Margaretta accepted one herself, all the while watching Miss Sweet, who was still pink with anger.

"It is no paradise," said Miss Sweet sharply. "The likes of Mr Fortescue ought not to be allowed in the door."

"Oh, is that so?" asked Louisa-Margaretta, smiling.

But Mrs Daw shook her head. "The behavior of many in the Beefsteak Club was rather objectionable. However, Miss Byrd makes very certain that those who support the theatre may not expect anything more than simple politeness from the actresses."

"They are anything but polite to *us*," said Miss Sweet. Then she looked at Dorothy. "It is quite different with Mr Beecham. I mean no offense to your cousin, you must understand."

Dorothy was savoring each sip of the fine tea, and it was plainly with effort that she turned her mind back to the conversation.

"My cousin?" she asked absently. "Whyever would any of my cousins be offended? I can assure you Mr Beecham is no relation."

"I'm sorry," said Miss Sweet, and indeed, she looked quite remorseful.

Louisa-Margaretta would have laughed if she, too, had not felt some tiny stirring of remorse. *Poor Judith!* Already, the more observant young ladies around them were connecting Judith's name to Mr Beecham's. If Louisa-

Margaretta did not separate the two of them soon, they would be considered engaged. At best, Mr Beecham would be seen as a gentleman who paid a lady great attention with no intention of proposing marriage, and he would not appreciate the reputation.

"Is there a different theatre where Mr Fortescue's behavior might have been... shall we say less restrained?" asked Louisa-Margaretta.

For the first time, Mrs Daw raised her eyebrows. "Really, Miss Haddington, I'm not sure how any of our actors will be helped by our speaking ill of the dead."

"But that is the only way to get at the truth," said Louisa-Margaretta.

Still, Mrs Daw continued to wave her questions away. "Truth! What is truth? We theatre ladies have a different perception than you do, I suppose."

Louisa-Margaretta sighed in frustration, but before she could continue the argument, a well-dressed young lady swept into the room.

"Good morning," said Miss Wynn. "I did not realise we were expecting such a party."

Mrs Daw cleared her throat, shooting a worried look from one young lady to the other.

Miss Sweet turned her face away, and her smile transformed itself into a sneer so quickly that Louisa-Margaretta could scarce believe it.

"It does not follow that you are welcome at this party," she snapped. "Miss St Clair and Miss Haddington came to see *me*, I believe."

"You could also do us the very great honour of leaving, Miss Sweet," said Miss Wynn. "Does not the duke require your company?"

Louisa-Margaretta felt sure Mrs Daw would intervene. If

nothing else, the two ladies under her care were being exceedingly rude to their guests.

But she only smiled and nodded. "That will do, girls," she said absently. "I must go find my hat."

Louisa-Margaretta recognised the dismissal, and she rose to take her leave because she knew it was expected. But she was terribly disappointed that she had not gotten to ask Miss Wynn anything about her thoughts. And she wondered whether, perhaps, it would be better for her to find the actress later, at the theatre.

Mrs Daw was bustling about, securing her hat quickly and pulling on a pair of gloves that were plain but still fashionable.

"Now," she said. "Shall we go see the funeral procession?"

37

———

Judith took care to be standing close enough to the appointed church at the hour Mr Fortescue's funeral ended. Though women were generally considered too "delicate" to attend funerals, she had helped her father prepare for enough of them that she was very familiar with how the service would go. And when the men began leaving the church, following a large and elaborate coffin, she knew how to find a part of the street where she could keep a respectful distance while still looking at each face.

The men from the Beefsteak Club were there, of course, though they were less identifiable when not in their uniforms. Mr Cartwright and Mr Beecham both looked suitably mournful, though Mr Hartsock seemed to take an unseemly pleasure in the pomp of the rituals. If he were indeed about to become a rich man, perhaps that was no surprise. And even Mr Beecham, when he touched his hat on seeing Judith, brightened rather unbecomingly. Judith shrank back.

Mr Fortescue seemed to have a great many friends or at least a good party of acquaintances. But there was nobody who appeared to be family. Though Judith looked at the faces of the mourners for some sign of familial resemblance or perhaps of great sorrow, she could not find one.

All the actors from *Così fan tutte* had come, which Judith thought curious. Louisa-Margaretta believed everyone from the theatre ought to attend so as to cast suspicion away from themselves. If Jasper failed to show up, for example, Mr Fudge might make note and decide he was a murderer.

Judith had argued with Jasper on that point, stating that he ought not to involve himself in any way, but he was walking slowly along with Mr Daw and Mr Nightingale. The faces of all three were appropriately somber, and Mr Nightingale seemed especially pale in the hot summer sun. Mr Daw, though serious, did not appear greatly distressed. But then, Judith could not easily have said what the emotions were in the heart of any of the three men. They were actors, and one glimpse of Mr Daw's villainous grin or Jasper's lovesick smile was enough to convince any theatre-goer that their characters were real. Yet at the end of the opera, the costumes came off, and all three went back to being their ordinary selves again.

The number of people was overwhelming. Judith thought back, in a flash, to her mother's death then wondered about her own funeral—where it would be held, who the mourners would be, and more importantly, who the women, left at home because of their assumed weakness, wearing black and grieving together, would be. *Would I have a daughter among them? Would Miriam still be living?*

After that, she thought of Morgan's funeral. And as soon as the thought was in her head, she couldn't breathe. She had been so sure, all along, that he was alive, but every person who thought her a fool leaped into her head. There were the Cluetts, soft in their English stoicism, hardly believing that she would go back to London under the circumstances; Madame Chatel, who encouraged her not to make such decisions based on the fate of any man; Mademoiselle Chatel, who wept in private when she assumed Judith couldn't hear; and Louisa-Margaretta, who put on a determined smile every time Judith spoke of Morgan but never mentioned him herself.

Even Jasper and Dorothy, kind though they were, had dropped plenty of hints about Judith being welcome to stay on with them in London. Considering the limited nature of their funds as well as the already-cramped accommodations, that could only be because they assumed Judith would be a widow.

Though she would not be a widow, of course. She and Morgan had never married. People might look askance on her wearing black for so much as a fortnight, let alone a year. Thinking for the first time of the likelihood that he had died, Judith felt as if she would need to wear black each day for the rest of her life.

She found that she could not move at all. People were walking all about her on the pavement, some with rude exclamations. One young man even called Judith a word she would have blushed to repeat simply because she was standing in his way. But she still found that she couldn't take a single step.

"We can hire a carriage," said Louisa-Margaretta. She had appeared, pink-cheeked from the heat, without Judith noticing. "But, Judith, you will need to walk. What has come over you?"

"I should have married Morgan when I had the chance," said Judith faintly. "That first spring, as soon as he told me the truth about his religion. I threw him over, and instead, we could have married. Everything would be different now."

Judith was aware of Louisa-Margaretta touching her and saying things, but instead, she was lost in her memories.

Her love for Morgan had been pure and open that first spring, her natural caution tempered with the knowledge that marriage was certainly his intention. And when he was finally able to be honest with her, confessing that he was a Quaker and not a member of her faith, the love itself did not diminish. Though grief settled over it like a pall, Judith was forced to break off the engagement.

As soon as she saw Morgan again, she knew she had made a mistake. Reencountering him confirmed for her the futility of trying to make any other arrangements for her life. She would never again meet anyone so intelligent, so easily able to understand her, and so respectful of her mind and her spirit. Indeed, most gentlemen fell short in the most laughable manner.

Judith would never laugh again, of course.

Some smelling salts were thrust beneath her nose, and Judith felt her legs beginning to move. Louisa-Margaretta was trying to lead her to the corner. In spite of the smelling salts, Judith could hardly take a breath. Louisa-Margaretta slipped coins to a pair of young boys, and they ran ahead, eager to get a carriage for the sort of ladies who might have even more coins to spare.

"He should not have gone to Vienna," said Judith vaguely. "Only he couldn't help but go there, not when he knew what was at stake. But I should have gone with him!"

Louisa-Margaretta laid a firm hand on Judith's shoulder.

"You were helping me because I needed you. And now you need to rest, Judith."

"I need no such thing. I need to find Morgan's grave."

But as soon as she was in the carriage, the world went dark.

38

Louisa-Margaretta deposited Judith at home, where she sank into the bed, having stumbled in from the carriage, and closed her eyes again. As Louisa-Margaretta hated sickbeds, she went out again immediately.

She went to the market, which was a bit of a novelty. Louisa-Margaretta had never needed to bargain for food in her life, and she was curious to see Dorothy plant her feet in front of a man selling potatoes.

"That'll be four shillings, miss," he said.

"Surely not," said Dorothy. "For such a quantity? It would be robbery to give you three shillings for this, but as I am in a hurry, you may have it."

"Not a chance. Four shillings it must be. You'll not find it for less."

Dorothy hesitated, and Louisa-Margaretta could see that she secretly must have agreed with the assessment. She wanted the potatoes but was loath to part with the money. For the first time, Louisa-Margaretta thought about what it must be like for Dorothy to have to economize with her brother's money. While Jasper was out late each night, no doubt dining and drinking with other theatrical types, his sister was counting every coin to make sure they could eat. And she was feeding two guests in the bargain, albeit with small meals and weak tea, with only a very little amount of help from a hired girl.

And for all that, she was terrible at bargaining.

"I'll give you exactly what the lady offered, but triple the quantity," said Louisa-Margaretta. She held out a sovereign while the old man glared, then put it directly into his palm before he could change his mind. The man snatched it then thrust a great deal of potatoes at Dorothy.

As they walked away, Dorothy said, "We didn't need half so many," sagging under the weight of her basket."

"It doesn't matter," said Louisa-Margaretta. "They will keep. Even I know that, and I'm not fond of potatoes."

Dorothy looked about. "I don't suppose you came here to buy vegetables."

Louisa-Margaretta sniffed. "No, not exactly."

"Why, then?"

Louisa-Margaretta observed the bustling crowd at the market. Her exchange with the potato man had been comparatively quiet. People were yelling everywhere, debating over both prices and quantity. There was even a rather elegant stall where a man was using a scale to weigh carrots, while onlookers jeered over this complicated system.

It felt odd to speak of her true purpose. Though Louisa-Margaretta was never one to hold her tongue, when she gossiped, she always had the sensation of causing a scandal. But there, she could say what she liked, and nobody would take much notice.

"It's Judith," she said. "I have been neglecting her, trying to save your brother, and now she is in a very bad way."

Dorothy's concern was genuine. "Was she taken ill? Has something happened?"

Louisa-Margaretta sighed. "No, nothing has happened, and that is the trouble. Not a single soul in London has been willing to help look for my cousin Morgan, and I have given Judith no assistance."

Dorothy did not look surprised. "That was very wrong of you."

"Of course it was," snapped Louisa-Margaretta. "She only came to London because she thought she could convince someone here to go to France and find him. Or Prussia. I have no idea. None of us can be sure whether he made it as far as France, though there were rumours that the Viscount Rialton had dined in some village there. Anyway, if not for that, she might have stayed in Russia or at least gone directly home to Derbyshire."

"Do you consider it home, then?"

Louisa-Margaretta thought for a moment. For years, she had despised Derbyshire, feeling like a princess trapped in a tower when her parents took her to Wycliff Castle to ensure that she broke off her engagement with Isaac.

But after the years she had spent there, she realised it *was* her home. And Judith's family was no small part of that.

"Yes. And we both need to return there. But not without —" She couldn't speak for a moment. She had wanted to say, "Not without Morgan," but that did not reflect her fears. Unlike Judith, Louisa-Margaretta did not have any belief that God would extract Morgan from France somehow. It was possible he had died there many months ago, and though she tried never to think of that, she had long ago accepted the possibility that Judith was only beginning to consider.

"We must know what happened to him," she said, her voice unsteady. "And where he has been laid to rest."

For a moment, Dorothy said nothing. Then she nodded. "Miss Haddington, you know that I live in London but have few connections here. My father's business has been relatively prosperous, but we have no influence on the sort of men who could, well, discover your cousin's whereabouts, And I am very sorry, but I cannot go to France myself or ask this of my brother."

"That does not concern me in the least," said Louisa-Margaretta. "But you can still do one thing that will help Judith a great deal."

Dorothy balanced the heavy basket of potatoes, carrots, and herbs on her hip. She was beginning to sweat in the hot sun, and she peered at Louisa-Margaretta with suspicion. "For Judith, anything. Only tell me what I must do."

39

The Fudge family had secured a box for the opening night of *Così fan tutte*. Louisa-Margaretta, taking full advantage of her standing as an old friend of the family, secured invitations for herself, Judith, and Dorothy to join that family in their box. It was funny how the title of "old friend" could seem in itself redolent almost of blackmail. Louisa-Margaretta, by virtue of her acquaintance with the family, knew things that they would not wish to have made public. They most likely knew many such stories about the Haddingtons as well. Yet it was easy to just pretend to maintain an uncomplicated friendship.

Mr Solier's comic opera was not going to be performed straightaway. Rather, the actors would have a few more days to learn it, then the theatre would promote its debut. That seemed utterly reasonable to Louisa-Margaretta, but her fiancé had decided it was unacceptable to him. He stayed away from the performance, insisting that his evening would be much better spent in creating new compositions than in tolerating the inferior work of Mr Mozart.

The beautiful new gown Louisa-Margaretta had

commissioned for Judith would have looked ghastly if she had worn it to the opera. She looked well in it ordinarily, but tonight, her eyes were dull, her complexion almost grey. Indeed, Judith had hardly risen from her bed all day. A decade ago, Louisa-Margaretta would have had nothing to do with such an individual. All she knew was that she was not allowed to stay in bed after breakfast. Mama never permitted such a thing.

But hard experience with women who were considered mad had strengthened Louisa-Margaretta's ability to cope. She knew how to dress, feed, and cajole a person who was reluctant to engage with any part of the world. Thus, with Dorothy's help, she got Judith in the carriage and to the opera. It was hardly worth the trouble, but she couldn't leave Judith alone in those ghastly hot rooms. And if the killer made another attempt, which Louisa-Margaretta considered a genuine possibility, she would need Judith's help.

Perhaps a murder would keep Judith from weeping—or sleeping. Those seemed just about the only two actions she was capable of at the moment.

"What a lovely evening," said Louisa-Margaretta, fanning herself against the heat. The Fudge family was certainly rather odd. Miss Fudge was home, supposedly with a sick headache, though Judith imagined it was because she found the opera dull. The grandmother, Mrs Stone, glared at the stage as if the immorality of the actors were going to infect her from afar. The cousin, Miss Russ, looking like a child in her elegant dress, picking at the lace on the sleeve and starting at every loud sound from the orchestra. Mr Felton Fudge, the only one of them who seemed to be enjoying the overture, was alternately attentive and shy.

Well, any port in a storm. At least in that setting, nobody would be likely to notice Judith's sorry state or bother her about it. Indeed, one of the first moments of compassion she ever saw from the Fudge ladies happened just as Judith was beginning to sway in her seat.

"There, now," said Mrs Stone. "Jenny, pass me the smelling salts, please."

"What she ought to have is a glass of brandy," said the young woman, and Louisa-Margaretta could not keep herself from laughing, even though her laugh rose above the music in the first moment when the audience was beginning to quieten. Jasper and Miss Wynn had entered the stage, and both were singing most eloquently of their love. Jasper's voice was not quite as pure and lovely as the other fellow's, but his expressions were much more pleasing.

"Mr Fudge, perhaps you might secure some refreshments for my friend," Louisa-Margaretta said, and both the gentlemen looked at her.

She had forgotten to address them properly. When she had first met Mr Felton Fudge, he had been just a young boy, and he still looked youthful to her eyes. He had the innocence of a happy child but also the speed and rose to his feet more quickly than his father. By the time Mr Christmas Fudge had looked about them, his son had already spoken to a footman, slipped him a generous amount of money, and secured a promise of fruit and beverages for all the ladies.

"Thank you," said Judith, and all the ladies started in surprise. The invalid could speak.

But Louisa-Margaretta was not shocked. She knew as well as anyone that music could be transporting, even for someone in such a sorry state as Judith, and that anyone who ignored its power was a fool.

Indeed, for the first act, Louisa-Margaretta herself was enchanted. The actresses were all superb, and one could sense the genuine affection between Mr and Mrs Daw as they pretended to plot together. The grandmother and young girl leaned closer to the rail, interested in spite of themselves. Only Dorothy and Mr Felton Fudge continued to converse, showing very little excitement even during the best part of the performance. Louisa-Margaretta supposed that attending so many performances, with only the barest acknowledgement from her brother, had made Dorothy rather tired of the whole enterprise.

Mr Christmas Fudge sometimes peered down at the stage, but he also seemed rather inattentive throughout. Louisa-Margaretta was thankful that he didn't attempt to speak to her. In fact, he was almost completely silent until he leaned over her chair at the beginning of the first intermission.

"I may not return," said the elder Fudge with quiet sincerity. "Please convey my respectful apologies to everyone in your party, Miss Haddington."

Louisa-Margaretta took one of the small plates of fruit. The stage looked remarkably dull, the curtains drawn. She always hated that part of the opera, when it seemed like an endless parade of people who were satisfied with their money and status. Louisa-Margaretta had taken care to wear a very elegant gown, of course, and though she did not travel with jewels, her long, reddish-golden hair was in an impeccably elegant arrangement. But she didn't stoop so low as to admit she was noticing what others were wearing. That would be unbecoming of a lady.

A gentleman in the box next to them shared no such qualms. He looked at a young, lovesick couple in a box opposite them and scoffed to his wife. "What people wear to the opera these days. It is rather sickening. In my day, one was expected to dress for the occasion. Now, even on the eve of war, young people think nothing of such disrespect. Mind you, I blame that Beau Brummell."

Louisa-Margaretta didn't think the clothing one chose for the unimpressive act of sitting in an opera box had a great deal to do with the war in France, and she was on the verge of saying something to the gentleman when his wife spoke.

"Well, the young people look to be quite taken with each other. And if you'll forgive me, I suppose an opinion of an old codger across the theatre must mean very little to them, although I'm sure they would be impressed by the lack of breeding indicated by such an open expression of your innermost thoughts, my dear," she said, with a twinkling smile.

Louisa-Margaretta stared at the lady with admiration, trying to remember if she had seen her before.

"If you feel strongly about it, my dear," the wife continued, her tone still one of bemusement, "I did see the magistrate in the other box. Mr Fudge, you know, the one who is incorruptible. Perhaps you could have the young people arrested."

Louisa-Margaretta was on her feet. "Judith, come with me. We've got to get to the green room."

40

They arrived just as Mr Christmas Fudge, accompanied by two other gentlemen, was walking out with Mr Daw.

"How dare you!" Miss Sweet shouted after them, but none of them acknowledged her in any way. Judith couldn't help noting that it was probably a singular experience for the young actress. Miss Sweet, beautiful and talented, would not be accustomed to gentlemen who took it upon themselves to ignore her.

She and Louisa-Margaretta went into the green room, where Miss Byrd confirmed the worst.

"They think Mr Daw did it," she said. "That Mr Fudge was just waiting to arrest him, making sure he would be here."

"And trying to ruin our performance in the process," said Jasper, his bitter tone almost unrecognisable. "He certainly delighted in humiliating all of us."

Judith noticed that in the commotion, the old rivalries and alliances were all falling away. The group stood as one. Mr Nightingale had his arm around Mrs Daw's shoulder, and though her face was stern, she was leaning on him. The other arm, he had given to Miss Sweet, who, Judith was amazed to see, had clasped Miss Wynn's hand tightly in hers. Jasper was at the end of the little party, holding tight to Miss Wynn as Miss Byrd stood before them.

As always in such moments, a Psalm came to Judith. But in deference to the company, she didn't speak. She only repeated the words in her mind. *The Lord is my shepherd. I shall not want.*

And for the first time since she had admitted to herself that Morgan would probably not return from his trip to the continent, she felt the possibility of survival. She did not feel hope, exactly, or the sense that she would ever be well. But her faith, a constant in her life from the beginning, reminded her that she could call on the Lord and that she might not be struck down with her dearest love. Rather, her life, in some greatly altered form, might possibly continue.

That faith, however, was not something she could impart to the actors. In fact, Mrs Daw was the only one of them who did not have tears in her eyes, though she seemed unable to speak.

Miss Byrd, who was the most fluttery of the whole company, spoke in a voice much sterner than any Judith had ever heard. "Mr Daw shall return to us. And he shall come back to either an opera that has failed or one that has risen above the scandal to become the greatest success in all London."

"How can we succeed without someone to play his part?" asked Jasper. "I know you said we couldn't afford to hire another gentleman until the show was proven a success, but now we have nobody at all."

"You have me," said Miss Byrd. "I pretended to be a

gentleman the other day, and I suppose I shall have to do it again tonight."

Miss Sweet gave a high-pitched, wild laugh. Miss Wynn only gasped.

Louisa-Margaretta was the first to speak. "Dear Miss Byrd, you have said yourself that you cannot act."

"Yes, and I shall be a laughingstock. But there is nothing for it, I'm afraid."

Louisa-Margaretta grinned. "Thanks to my friend Judith's tireless efforts, I know the libretto rather well. Let me go on in dear Mr Daw's place. I shall have to take his part up an octave, but I daresay I could get the character right."

41

———

The champagne was flowing in the ladies' dressing room. All the women crowded around Louisa-Margaretta, who had taken the most comfortable chair, and Miss Wynn could hardly keep from laughing. Miss Byrd had had rather too many glasses of the French wine, and Miss Sweet's lovely smile was at its most radiant. Even Mrs Daw appeared rather less wooden, although sadness filled her eyes.

"My dear husband will be most impressed when we tell him of this, Miss Haddington," she said. "Indeed, he will consider you quite a threat. How is he to make his living now?"

Louisa-Margaretta smiled then took a great swig of the wine, which burned her throat. "I never thought it would be quite so exhilarating. What is a drawing room compared to a stage?"

"But will it not cause a great scandal for you?" asked Miss Wynn. "I beg your pardon, but ladies of your sort are not generally permitted to be actresses."

Louisa-Margaretta gave a merry laugh. "Of course

they're not. Which is why I have never in my life acted in anything, not once."

Miss Sweet started, "But you—"

"I'm sure you will agree, dear Angel," Mrs Daw said. "And that both you ladies, when asked about the marvelous actress who took my husband's place on the stage, will express amazement that a stranger who happened to know the libretto appeared. What a pity we never quite caught her name."

Louisa-Margaretta laughed. "At least that part of it can be explained away. Judith would have known every word, especially those revised sections, but I didn't quite have it all. I'm sure many in the audience could hear Miss Byrd prompting me."

Miss Wynn was looking at Louisa-Margaretta, curious. "Do you think you've missed your calling then, Miss Haddington? Would you have liked to be on the stage?"

Louisa-Margaretta considered, taking a slower sip of the wine, which was harsh against her tongue, and her extraordinarily red lips left a mark on the glass.

"I do enjoy acting," she said. "But it has been called for in so many parts of my life, not simply on the stage. I suppose I enjoy finding something that demands I use my wits. The stage would suit, of course, but so would many other things."

In spite of the camaraderie she felt with the ladies, she could not add anything about how she enjoyed finding out murderers. That was generally the most exciting use for her gifts. But any lady of the *haut ton* had to pretend a good deal of emotions she did not necessarily feel, so perhaps they thought she was just speaking of the life of a well-born daughter.

And, indeed, she soon had an opportunity to prove it.

Judith burst through the door, breathing heavily. Her face was pale, though she still looked much healthier than the wan young woman who had been dragged to the Fudge family's box only hours ago.

"Louisa-Margaretta," she said. "Your parents have just arrived."

"*What?* But it is so very late. Have they been in London all day? They would not have traveled in the dark, I'm sure."

"They were waiting for hours, apparently. But they learned you would be at the theatre, and they have just come. I don't think they saw any of the performance, but we must hurry."

42

I t took three actresses, one director, and all of Judith's panicked ministrations to get Louisa-Margaretta back into the gown she had worn for the performance. Her hair, which had been rearranged to fit beneath a wig, looked absolutely awful.

"We have no time to make it look decent," said Miss Sweet.

"I can't go out like this," said Louisa-Margaretta, her voice growing thinner with each moment.

Judith thought for a minute. "Do any of you ladies have a turban?"

Miss Wynn snapped her fingers. "No. I have something better."

She found a wig, a plain but respectable one in a shade of dull brown that was almost identical to Judith's hair.

"Here," she said. "Say you wore it to avoid unwelcome attention from the gentlemen here."

In her original gown, wearing the unbecoming wig, Louisa-Margaretta crept out of the room with Judith. The latter saw too late that there was a streak of white paint to the side of Louisa-Margaretta's left ear, but it was too late to remove it.

"Darling," said Mrs Haddington, rushing to embrace her daughter.

Mr Haddington appeared overcome, though as always, he was quiet. He embraced Louisa-Margaretta, nodded to Judith, then looked utterly flummoxed by all the emotions about him.

"Lou," he said, "Miss St Clair. Wonderful to have you back."

"Yes, it is good to see you, Miss St Clair," said Mrs Haddington with cold formality. Then in a slightly less hostile tone, she added, "Your family was all well when we left Derbyshire."

Judith, thankful for that small mercy, gave her quavering thanks. She had hoped Mrs Haddington might be partly pleased with her. After all, Louisa-Margaretta had returned from Russia with a fiancé, someone her family would at least not find objectionable. But it seemed Mrs Haddington would not easily forgive Judith, no matter what the circumstances.

Still, she was certainly interested in the gentleman. He was the first person she asked about after she offered a brief thanks to the Lord for bringing her daughter back across the ocean safely. "We were hoping to meet Mr Solier. Is he not here?"

"No," said Louisa-Margaretta, stealing a glance at Judith. "Was he not with his hosts?"

"He was not," said her mama. But her training in avoiding any awkwardness or implication of scandal served her well, and she added, "Perhaps he had plans of which we were all unaware."

"Surprised he didn't come down to the opera," added Mr

Haddington. It reminded Judith that Louisa-Margaretta's father was quiet but far from unobservant.

"We had quite a crowd as it was," Louisa-Margaretta said. "We were in a box with some friends."

"Which friends?" asked Mrs Haddington quickly.

It reminded Judith that for Louisa-Margaretta, the rules had changed. In St Petersburg, the only supervision she'd had was from her ineffectual English hosts and a shrewd old French emigree, a woman who believed that Louisa-Margaretta's lack of occupation was much more troubling than her spinsterhood.

In England, especially with her parents in close proximity, Louisa-Margaretta's freedom would be greatly curtailed.

"Old friends of yours, Mama," said Louisa-Margaretta sweetly. "Mr Christmas Fudge, Mr Felton Fudge, the young man's grandmother, and a relation of their family. Miss Russ, a young girl who is only just out." Otherwise, Mrs Haddington might suspect any visiting cousin of being male and unattached. "Though the elder Mr Fudge was called away by, well, business."

"In the middle of an opera," said Mrs Haddington, shaking her head.

"They were very kind," said Judith primly. She didn't wish to let the conversation stray to the subject of Mr Fudge's business. Already, it would be difficult to keep Dorothy quiet on the subject of the murder and the way Mr Fudge had treated Jasper, though Judith suspected the arrest of Mr Daw might placate her for a moment.

She hardly had time to wonder what had become of Dorothy before her friend tried to steer the elder Haddingtons away from the green room.

"I'm not sure the rest of the Fudge family has left," said

Louisa-Margaretta hastily. "I can show you their box if you'd like."

"Oh, dear little Felton," said her mother. "Though I suppose he would like to be called Mr Fudge now himself. He was always such a guileless child."

"We'll be back in a moment, Judith," said Louisa-Margaretta.

"Oh, darling," her mother said as they were leaving. "What is this on your cheek?"

After only a moment's pause, Louisa-Margaretta said airily, "I suppose it comes from embracing all these actresses. The amount of paint they have to put on their faces, Mama, you would scarce believe it!"

"Indeed," said her mother. "Well, dear, hand me a handkerchief. I'll help you get it off."

43

———

As soon as the Haddingtons departed, the green room filled with cast members again. Mrs Daw had begun to look tired, Miss Wynn, determined, and Miss Sweet, troubled. The two gentlemen both looked rather ill. In fact, Mr Nightingale was lying on the couch, clutching a bucket Jasper had brought.

"It must be nerves, surely," said Miss Sweet. "This evening was trying for all of us."

She winced as Mr Nightingale leaned over the bucket, bringing up almost nothing from his stomach but sounding as if he were very ill indeed.

"Did you smoke one of the cigars?" Judith asked Jasper. "Are those the same ones you used in rehearsals?"

"We don't light them in rehearsals," snapped Miss Byrd, looking ill herself at the thought of losing yet another actor before the second performance. "We can't afford to waste money in that manner."

"I don't light them at all," confessed Jasper. "I can never manage to fiddle with the matchsticks while singing, and I think the audience hardly notices."

"I didn't notice at all," said Judith distantly. But her mind was elsewhere. The cigars had not been touched for some time, then—not since the night Mr Fortescue died.

"I must go speak with Louisa-Margaretta," she said, rising to her feet so quickly that she nearly knocked over the bucket.

Mrs Daw had the presence of mind to grab it, thus ensuring that the green room floor was free from the contents of Mr Nightingale's stomach. "What is it, dear?" she asked. "Shall I go with you?"

Judith considered. "No. I can go alone. Besides, someone has to care for Mr Nightingale, and you're the only one with the stomach for it. I do think he should see a doctor, though. Or at least someone who has experience dealing with poison."

"Poison?" asked Miss Wynn, unsteady.

Judith was sure she wasn't acting. She looked as if she were going to collapse. Jasper held her up, and Judith was glad to see that he could help someone who was merely emotional, though he was not much good with his genuinely sick friend.

"Yes," said Judith. "I'll explain later."

44

The Fudge family had left when Louisa-Margaretta reached the box with her parents, and there was no sign of Dorothy. Though the theatre liked for people to stay, spending money and gossiping after the performance, many of the patrons were already gone. Louisa-Margaretta suspected they would all be eager to spread gossip about the performance in the morning. She gave a small, triumphant smile, realising that none of her parents' acquaintances would ever believe she'd been the one playing Don Alfonso.

But there was some trouble ahead, for they ran into Mr Solier.

"Ah, Miss Haddington," he said in brisk French, not appearing to notice her parents. "I have altered some of the revisions. Your Mr Coleman, he is worse than I thought. Either the man is mad, or English sensibilities are the most delicate in all the civilized world."

Louisa-Margaretta's father stifled a smile, which galled her. It was hardly the introduction she might have hoped for.

"Mama, Papa," she said. "May I present Mr Solier. Mr Solier, my parents."

She didn't call him her intended or her fiancé. After all, her parents already knew of the relationship between them.

"Mr Solier, such a pleasure!" her mother said. "I'm sorry to hear that the revisions were not to your taste."

"Oh," he said, unsure how to respond. "Well, Miss St Clair, she was hard at work. But she has no experience in these matters."

"One learns by doing," said Louisa-Margaretta's father, peering at Mr Solier with skepticism he did not fully disguise. "And Miss St Clair learns exceptionally quickly."

Mrs Haddington shot her husband a stern look, and Louisa-Margaretta burned with annoyance. Her parents, usually so warm and affectionate with one another, were arguing within a minute of meeting Mr Solier. Though they didn't agree on the subject of Judith's influence, that was still an unusual outcome and not at all a desirable one. *How are we all to spend any time together in Wycliff Castle if we cannot manage this first meeting?*

"Come," she said briskly. "I'm sure you are all tired. Let us collect dear Judith, then we may all retire for the night. The revisions will surely look better in the morning."

45

Judith knew why Mr Beecham had asked to speak to her in the music room. And with all the commotion backstage and the door standing wide open, she could hardly refuse. She knew from experience that a refusal would not help. When men like Mr Beecham were determined to ignore a lady's feelings, unwilling to see the hesitation in her eyes or hear the indifference in her tone, no amount of waiting would help them see the error of their ways. The only possible option was a direct and immediate refusal, one that Judith was perfectly willing to give.

When the gentleman did not speak right away, Judith began with the intent of making the conversation a short one.

"Mr Beecham," she said. "I must apologise to you. I'm afraid that by my words or actions or perhaps both, I have given a false impression."

"Dear Miss St Clair!" he cried. "You have done nothing wrong, of course! Nothing! But from our first conversation, it has struck me that you are one of the finest women I have ever had the privilege to know."

"Please, Mr Beecham, I cannot let you make such a speech. If you are intending to make an offer, please accept my best wishes, but under no circumstances would I be able to accept."

"Perhaps I ought to speak of my friends," he continued quickly. "You've seen for yourself that Hartsock and Cartwright are like brothers to me. But neither of them is happy, and I put this down to the want of a proper wife."

"Well—"

"Cartwright ought to marry. It is all drink, amusement, and cards with him. That may do well enough for a younger man, but now that we're all of a rather more advanced age, I must say it is not terribly becoming."

Judith didn't find a dissolute and aimless life becoming in any man, but she didn't say so.

"And poor Hartsock is unhappy in marriage, so he is not the one whose course I should hope to follow either."

"I'm not sure it is our place to comment on the Hartsocks' union," said Judith with as much disapproval in her voice as she could muster, but Mr Beecham ignored her.

"Oh, the lady is blameless, to be sure! Only they are not well suited. You must see that. He enjoys friends and society, and she wants to keep him always in the country, which for him is dull. She could manage the estate well enough on her own, with the assistance of the men Hartsock has hired, but she is always trying to drag him into those petty matters when he has an artistic soul. He wants to write an opera, you see."

"I suppose he ought to write one, then," said Judith, though she knew the discussion would be distracting. She should have kept her mind on Mr Beecham's declarations, only she felt compelled to defend poor Mrs Hartsock. And she had not been at all impressed with the husband. "He doesn't have a profession to occupy him, so I suppose he could spare the hours if he wished to. Mr Solier wrote more than one opera under conditions of exile and poverty, and even now, he writes between his obligations here in London."

Invoking Mr Solier's name was a mistake. Mr Beecham's face softened immediately.

"Ah, yes, that dear Frenchman! He is certainly accomplished. Your friend Miss Haddington appears most fortunate in her choice of husband, Miss St Clair, and I hope you will find yourself equally so."

"I have," said Judith sharply. At the thought of Morgan, her sympathy for Beecham evaporated. "I have received and accepted a proposal of marriage from Miss Haddington's cousin. In fact, I have been going about London, trying to find someone who genuinely wishes to help me find him."

Genuine feeling came to Mr Beecham's face, which only served to anger her.

"I am sorry," he said. "My understanding was that Mr Ramsbury had passed away and that this had become evident to you. If this is not the case—"

"It does not signify whether he is living or dead. For I have seen one example of a man whose mind and heart are perfectly suited to mine, and it is something I shall never be able to unsee, Mr Beecham. You must forgive me."

He did not look ready to forgive her. In fact, he didn't look at all prepared to accept her rejection, but at that moment, they were interrupted by Louisa-Margaretta's family. She, her parents, and Mr Solier were in the passageway, and Louisa-Margaretta smiled in relief as soon as she saw Judith.

46

———

Not until they were both dressed for bed, pretending to be tired and ready to sleep, did Judith finally have a chance to speak with Louisa-Margaretta. They talked in whispers so that neither Dorothy nor Jasper would hear them. They were seated together in the tiny parlor, Judith wrapped in her mother's old shawl, Louisa-Margaretta in an elegant nightdress. Judith knew that her friend was seldom cold, especially in summer.

"It was the cigars," said Judith. "I'm certain of it."

Louisa-Margaretta frowned. "Poisoned cigars? It seems like a rather terrible way of assuring oneself that Mr Fortescue would die."

But Judith was quite sure. "He loved to smoke cigars, and it was clear that he was going to stay for the whole rehearsal, smoking one after another."

"What became of those cigars, then?"

Judith gripped her friend's arm. "Don't you see? Miss Byrd kept them, as the theatre cannot afford to waste such an opportunity. Her father smoked one—or part of one—

and fell ill. Mr Nightingale took a few puffs of another, and he was ill as well though not as gravely."

Thoughtful, Louisa-Margaretta said, "So you can go and tell Mr Fudge. What then?"

Judith frowned. "I have to tell him. But I'm afraid it will not help us."

Louisa-Margaretta sighed. "Of course it will! You've solved it."

"No. This doesn't tell us who the poisoner was. And if Mr Fudge thinks it was Mr Daw, it could harm him."

Caught in the dilemma, Judith paused for a moment. Though she knew the law was far from fair, she could not in good conscience keep anything from an honest magistrate. But she also didn't imagine Mr Daw to be guilty, and she would never forgive herself if her discovery helped push the poor man to the scaffold.

"Oh, stop looking like a sad puppy, Judith. You needn't tell Mr Fudge anything. I absolve you. Just tell the actors not to smoke those cigars."

"That, I can certainly do," said Judith. "We should go to the theatre first thing in the morning."

"You may go. You rise earlier anyway."

"If you're not coming to the theatre with me, what will you do tomorrow?"

"I'm going to prepare for my wedding," said Louisa-Margaretta. "Oh, do join me, Judith, if only for the morning. Mama will insist on a special license, of course, so the wedding can take place immediately. The want of a proper trousseau will be the only delay."

Judith swallowed. For the first time, she comprehended the change. Louisa-Margaretta was soon going to be a married woman. The travels and adventures they had shared would be over. No longer could they be first in each other's thoughts. And while Judith had never taken the romantic view of friendship that some fashionable ladies espoused, she began to feel the loss.

"Oh, Judith, cheer up," said Louisa-Margaretta. "When I'm married, I shall need your company more than ever."

Judith gave a sad smile. "Not if you're in Europe."

"Well, that won't be possible unless the rumours of victory are true. Do you believe any of them?"

Judith shivered. "How can I when no official messenger has yet arrived? There are always rumours in times of war."

Louisa-Margaretta laughed. "Is this truly a time of war? Again?"

Judith frowned, thinking of what might have happened to Morgan in French territory. "Yes. And I am very much afraid it shall remain that way."

47

———

Mrs Norman, the shopkeeper who had been attentive to Louisa-Margaretta before, all but fell at her feet the next morning. Since her mama had arrived, eager to settle her debt and buy all sorts of new items for her trousseau, the shopkeeper and her assistant were ready to neglect all other customers in order to outfit the lovely young lady.

"What do you think of this material for a day dress?" asked Mrs Haddington. "Come, touch it, Louisa-Margaretta."

The latter, who was not feeling any joy in the process, touched a length of very fine muslin.

"It's not practical for the countryside," she said. "It would be perfectly muddy as soon as we set foot in Derbyshire. You know that, Mama."

Mrs Haddington blinked. "Well, surely you will be in London more often, my dear. Does not Mr Solier require a residence here? There are no opera houses anywhere near Wycliff Castle, as you well know."

Louisa-Margaretta sighed. "I have already gone months without riding."

The shopkeeper, no doubt used to the exact conversation, smiled as she interrupted. "Would the young lady be interested in a riding habit?"

"One can ride in London," said Mrs Haddington.

"Hardly," scoffed Louisa-Margaretta. "Urging a tired horse across a flat, weathered patch of brown grass is not the sort of riding that interests me. And it is so terribly hot just now."

"That is all anyone is speaking of," said the shopkeeper. "This abominable heat. And that business with the French, of course."

"I'm sure it ended in a victory, just as some are saying," said Mrs Haddington.

"Are you?" asked Louisa-Margaretta, fully prepared to argue with her mother about any subject—the war, the weather, the proper color for evening gloves. "I'm not at all sure. Napoleon Bonaparte was on Elba during the whole time the diplomats tried to divide the spoils of Europe, and they could not manage even that before he both escaped and raised an army."

That silenced her mother and the shopkeeper, which had been her aim. But Mrs Haddington never stayed silent for long.

"You have plenty of riding habits, dear," she said. "But you're going to need another gown for special events, especially since I'm sure your married life will involve many trips to the theatre."

As if summoned by the mention of that place, Judith arrived with Mrs Daw. The actress, who looked as if she'd aged a decade in one night, nearly fell on Louisa-Margaretta.

"Dear Miss Haddington," she said. "Miss St Clair said the two of you shall help me. I must find the responsible party before my husband is hanged!"

Mrs Haddington started. "Dear lady, this is hardly the time or place for such a conversation. My daughter is very busy at present with her trousseau –"

"And I am occupied in keeping my husband's neck out of the noose," snapped Mrs Daw with uncharacteristic venom. "So I should hope that my priorities are clear."

"Mrs Daw, please," said Judith.

Since Louisa-Margaretta knew Judith would be worried about giving Mama even more reasons for resentment, she stepped in. "I'm sure we can help you, Mrs Daw. I will make my purchases then call on you."

But Mrs Daw did not hear the dismissal. She simply stood, breathing heavily, looking between Judith and Louisa-Margaretta with all the blind panic of a cornered fox.

"Mrs Daw," said Judith. "I will speak to my friend. Please, go to your home and wait for us there."

Mrs Daw knew how to kill with a glare. Looking as if she would like to tear Mrs Haddington limb from limb, she rushed out of the shop.

Louisa-Margaretta knew that, within a few yards, the poor lady would certainly have to stop and cry.

48

———

Mrs Norman was too polite to comment on the scene, but Judith noticed that both Louisa-Margaretta and her mother were in a rush to leave after that. With promises to return, they ushered Judith out of the shop and down the street.

They were silent until they reached a ladies' tearoom and conversed in polite murmurs until they had been served. Judith almost laughed. If anyone in the room could have guessed the topic of their conversation, they would have been shocked. A handsome, well-dressed woman of great wealth, her beautiful daughter, and a plain but respectable friend sat at a perfectly lovely table. And over cake and rather excellent tea, they were discussing a murder.

Mrs Haddington, who was always well bred, kept her voice low.

"Really, Louisa-Margaretta, I'm surprised at you. You ought to be thinking about your trousseau, not meddling in this woman's business."

Judith took greedy sips of the tea, something she had

missed while staying so long with Jasper and Dorothy. To her dismay, she found she had grown rather used to the finest tea and china. Perhaps she was becoming a grand lady after all.

Of course, Louisa-Margaretta, her expression haughty with poorly concealed anger, looked much more regal than Judith could ever have managed.

"Because marriage is the only thing that could possibly be important to me," Louisa-Margaretta hissed.

"Because marriage *is* important," snapped Mrs Haddington. "It is an institution created by God, as you will hear yourself in the ceremony. It is not something to be taken as a joke."

"Oh, Mama, I do not consider my marriage with Mr Solier any sort of joke. If it's any consolation, we almost never laugh together."

She had chosen her barb well. Mrs Haddington looked stricken but only for a moment.

"If you're not serious about the marriage, this is the moment to reconsider. Better a broken engagement than a disastrous marriage."

"Yes, but better a marriage than a lifetime spent as a spinster. Or that is what you've led me to believe. Besides, as you have shown me, a broken engagement is not exactly amusing."

Louisa-Margaretta, as clever as she was, had not thought that insult through. Mrs Haddington quickly recovered her footing.

"Your previous fiancé was not suitable," she said. "His family agreed and wished to find him a Jewish bride. The engagement, as you call it, could never be serious on either side, and I will never understand why you insist on referring to a youthful dalliance as some sort of solemn promise."

They were silent for a moment. Louisa-Margaretta sipped her tea. Then she came up with a response.

"It *was* a solemn promise. And I cannot speak for the way Isaac abandoned me after. It was disgraceful." Her voice wavered. "But at the time we became engaged, had we not been separated by our families, I know he would have married me."

Judith was impressed. It was the first time she'd ever heard Louisa-Margaretta make such a definitive statement about her former beloved's intentions. For years, Louisa-Margaretta had agonized over Isaac's seeming indifference, and when she'd run into him and heard of his engagement to a lady in New York, her sorrow erupted into rage. But it heartened Judith to hear that Louisa-Margaretta, at least at one time, had felt Isaac's love to be perfectly sincere. She had known that moment of bliss then.

Mrs Haddington, perhaps seeing that she was losing her daughter's attention, tried a different tactic. "Come. Let us finish the plans for your wedding. You will have a husband and a place to stay, then you may think of calling on this woman tomorrow week."

"I have a place to stay already," Louisa-Margaretta said. "Miss St Clair and her brother will not turn me out."

Mrs Haddington's expression was decidedly sour. "They will if their uncle's patron wishes it."

Judith, against her wishes, gasped. Her father loved his position in Derbyshire. The tithes he received as rector were more than enough to support the family, else he would certainly struggle to settle money on Miriam and provide for his sons as they reached adulthood. He adored his parishioners, and he was kept from overwork because he was able to pay a curate. Losing the patronage of the Haddingtons would be devastating to him.

"Fine," snapped Louisa-Margaretta. "Even you, Mama, would not be so ridiculous as to take revenge on Judith's poor father simply because you are angry with me. I can stay with Mrs Daw. In fact, that is exactly what I shall do. Judith, do not get involved. Save your father's position, stay with your cousins, and when I have found the murderer, I'll send you word."

"Louisa-Margaretta," said Judith, "please, I beg you. There is no reason for you to rush away from me or from your mother."

Mrs Haddington was aghast. "What of the money your father intended to settle on you, Louisa-Margaretta? It would keep you and Mr Solier in comfort, and you would relinquish that?"

Louisa-Margaretta hesitated. She had only ever known a lifetime of wealth and abundance and could not have any idea what she was taking on by committing to a life of genteel poverty. And while Judith did not appreciate the bitter, weak tea she drank with Dorothy, the heat of the small rooms, or the many other necessities that were forced upon the household, at least she knew how to endure them. She'd been poor as a child, so she could manage living on very little as a woman.

"Of course I do not wish to relinquish it," she said. "But I cannot let them hang Mr Daw. And really, Mama, as you're a Christian woman, I'm quite surprised that you can countenance such a thing yourself."

Louisa-Margaretta left the tearoom as soon as she had put her gloves on, leaving her mother speechless.

"I'm sorry," said Mrs Haddington, though Judith wasn't sure what the apology was for. Perhaps she was simply sorry that a young woman she disliked had overheard such a personal conversation.

After a moment, Mrs Haddington said, "I am very fond of your father."

"We are in your debt," said Judith quickly, and she felt the pain of her position as she said the words. No matter how much money her father managed to put aside, they would always be dependent on the goodwill of a woman who presently disliked her.

The thought spurred her to act. "I am sorry as well, Mrs Haddington." She hoped her voice sounded respectful and not rushed. "And I very much hope I shall see you at your daughter's wedding."

49

———————

Louisa-Margaretta arrived at Mrs Daw's house in a state. She was surprised to find the lady had followed her instructions and was awaiting her there. With her were Miss Sweet, Miss Wynn, and the Duke of Ormonde. Even Mr Nightingale was present. The whole cast was assembled, apart from Jasper and poor Mr Daw.

"Good morning," she said. "Mrs Daw has asked me to find Mr Fortescue's killer, so I shall be brief. What have you all kept from me?"

The group was silent, confirming to Louisa-Margaretta that they shared a secret.

"Out with it, then."

Miss Sweet glared at her. "We know you're chummy with the magistrate and his family. So are the St Clairs. Why would we trust you?"

"My own cousin will be hanged for this murder if Mr Daw does not swing for it," she said, earning a gasp from Miss Sweet. "Besides, any one of you could ruin my reputation by mentioning that I took Mr Daw's place on the stage. So I should say we're even."

"That will do," said Mrs Daw. "My dear, if you would care to enlighten her?"

She turned not to Miss Sweet but to the other young actress.

Miss Wynn looked away. "My affections are engaged elsewhere, but I knew I should not marry. It's not beneficial to an actress who is not yet established, you see. For one like Mrs Daw, yes, but I have my own sort of reputation to maintain."

Louisa-Margaretta was trying to follow. "The reputation of a courtesan?"

The duke made to object, but Miss Wynn nodded.

"You have attended the theatre," she said. "You knew Mr Fortescue. For some of the men, actresses are only interesting if they are a sort of, well, prey. I'm sure you've heard all the rumours about our, well, fellow actress who keeps a box at another theatre in order to show off her beauty and seek out men who might... who—"

"Patrons of actresses have certain expectations," Mrs Daw filled in for her. "The Lyceum Theatre is more respectable, but even under Miss Byrd's supervision, men will be drawn to the theatre if there's a young woman there who is beautiful and unattached. When one is drawing crowds because of success rather than scandal, marriage becomes an option."

Louisa-Margaretta looked between Miss Wynn and Miss Sweet, realisation dawning on her at last.

"The two of you were not rivals," she said. "You had screaming battles in the streets for the crowds, not for love."

"Correct," said Miss Sweet. "Though I assure you it is a great compliment to us that you were convinced, Miss Haddington."

"And Jasper tried to give us all away, insisting that we

were virtuous young women!" said Miss Wynn. "I suppose he couldn't stand to hear us slandered. Fortunately, Mr Fudge didn't make too much of that."

Louisa-Margaretta looked at the duke, realising for the first time that he was sitting closer to Mr Nightingale than to Miss Sweet. It appeared that, as with Miss Wynn, his affections were engaged. Perhaps they had been for some time.

"Eventually, of course, I will marry," said the duke. "But I have to find the right sort of wife."

Mr Nightingale smirked. "Discretion in a wife is a quality that cannot be overvalued. I'm seeking the same sort of young woman myself."

"You would have better luck in Paris," said Louisa-Margaretta. "If any of us can ever go to Paris again, that is."

Mrs Daw sighed. "When I was looking for you, everyone was saying that Waterloo was victorious. But others say there has been no messenger yet. I don't know what to believe."

Louisa-Margaretta was solemn. "I know little of Napoleon Bonaparte, but Judith tells us that this war will last for some years yet. And I have no reason to disbelieve that."

"Paris after the war, then," said the duke. "Miss Sweet, perhaps we can continue our courtship until that time."

The young woman gave him her beautiful smile, and Louisa-Margaretta finally understood the innocent affection in her gaze.

"Of course, my darling," she said.

"That still leaves Mr Fortescue, though," said Louisa-Margaretta. "I may as well confess that I had met him before. He made some threats against my family, though he never followed through."

"What was the nature of the threats?" asked Mr Nightingale, but the duke gestured for silence. Louisa-Margaretta would not have revealed their nature in any case.

"He enjoyed saying he was going to reveal all sorts of things, and my family has its share of secrets," said Louisa-Margaretta, hoping that would satisfy them. "He wanted me to marry him."

Miss Wynn gasped. "But you came to London engaged to another man, and still, he did nothing."

"He would have," said Louisa-Margaretta.

But the duke shook his head. "No, he wouldn't. Mr Fortescue liked to prey on the weak. He threatened me for years, and I considered killing him myself."

He looked about, as if perhaps one of the young women would challenge him, but when nobody was surprised by his declaration, he chose to continue.

"Eventually, I told him to tell all and be damned. It was speculation anyway. I have always been very careful. And it would reflect just as poorly on him as it would on me, were he revealed to be the source. I was afraid for my life, but eventually, I was more afraid that I was turning over my soul to Mr Fortescue."

"And he did not," said Miss Sweet. "That was what you were always telling me about him."

"Yes. He was a vicious man, and he liked to see others suffer. But if he saw them as a threat to himself, whether because of their knowledge or something in their character, his words were always empty."

Louisa-Margaretta nearly cried. She had been taking Mr Fortescue's words seriously for many years, and they had caused her countless hours of pain. She had tried everything to escape from him, retreating not only to Derbyshire but also to Russia, hoping she could outrun both his infatuation and his animosity. And all that time, she had been in very little danger, as he must have sensed that she would fight him most viciously if he dared to go after her family.

But her character was strong. And at once, she knew the identity of the killer.

She nearly knocked over a little end table in her haste.

"We must leave at once!" she said. And even in a moment of panic, it gratified Louisa-Margaretta to see that the actors all intended to follow her.

50

———

J udith had removed the cigars from their place on a table behind the stage in the morning. But it had finally occurred to her that the killer wouldn't know the danger was past.

And when she interrupted the man, who had turned over the entire area in his search, she knew that her instincts for identifying murderers hadn't failed her.

"I had no idea you would be here," she said. "Why, everyone is so very occupied today, waiting for news of the war."

He was not fooled for a moment.

"I can't let you leave, Miss St Clair," he said. "Who else knows about me?"

Judith could only tell the truth. She could not possibly throw any of her friends or family members upon the mercy of this man, as much as she wished to save her own life.

"Nobody," she said quietly.

"Sit in this chair." He bound her tightly to it then piled as much cloth as he could around it. When he began lighting candles in the little candelabra that usually stood at the side of the stage, Judith's blood went cold.

"It will be quick," he said.

His regret appeared genuine, which only made Judith feel more panicked.

"There are so many candles here," he said. "If one starts a fire on the stage, that will come as a shock to nobody."

For a moment, Judith couldn't speak, not even to plead for her life. But she gathered her thoughts quickly.

"They will keep looking for you until they find out what happened to Mr Fortescue," she said weakly.

The killer smiled. "I believe that old actor killed him, Mr Daw. I spread that rumour, and it ended in an arrest. People may wonder about your death, but they will soon forget."

"And what about your death?" shouted someone from the other side of the stage.

Judith squinted in the candlelight, her eyes blurred with a sudden rush of tears, but she didn't need to see clearly in order to recognise Louisa-Margaretta.

The man took a step back. "Stay away. This theatre is about to burn."

"Not unless you're the only one in it." Louisa-Margaretta took no notice of the heavy candlestick as she walked up to Judith and undid the ropes with a few quick tugs.

"You should have used better knots," she said mockingly.

The killer threw the candlestick at Louisa-Margaretta before leaping backwards. It found its mark, though his aim was poor, and Louisa-Margaretta was only hit in the ankle. Still, she gave an involuntary gasp of pain.

Judith stood, weak on her feet. "Let us end this peacefully," she said to the man.

But he wasn't listening. He took another look at the candelabra.

Then another voice interrupted them. "Follow me!"

Judith couldn't see him clearly in the dim theatre, but she saw his cap bobbing as he ran and the killer following him.

"Judith, go!" said Louisa-Margaretta.

Louisa-Margaretta moved slowly, the place where the candlestick had connected with her ankle clearly giving her great pain. And Judith was hardly faster. Try as they might, they couldn't keep up.

The killer, who had gambled so rashly and so often that he was greatly in Mr Fortescue's debt, had risked everything one last time. And he appeared to have won.

Both men left through the rear door of the theatre. Judith heard it opening, then she heard Mr Cartwright's cry of surprise.

By the time she hobbled over, Mr Cartwright had his arms held by Miss Sweet and Miss Wynn, while Miss Byrd took a length of twine from the pocket of her jacket and began to bind them. She had spoken with such a convincingly masculine voice, hearing her real voice was a great shock.

"Not to worry, dear Miss St Clair," she said, "I know how to tie a very good knot."

51

In a matter of moments, Mr Nightingale and Mrs Daw joined the party. They had been posted at the entrance to the theatre, where Louisa-Margaretta had thought Mr Cartwright might emerge, and were disappointed to have missed all the action.

Actors, as it turned out, could never get quite enough drama.

The Duke of Ormonde, red-faced, was following with Mr Fudge. Three of Mr Fudge's young men rushed over to the prisoner, taking over from the actresses, who relinquished him with great reluctance.

"I found your Mr Fudge just leaving his home," the duke said to Louisa-Margaretta. "You were quite right, though. My poor horses are exhausted."

Louisa-Margaretta gave Mr Fudge a curious smile. "Why were you leaving, then?"

"I was coming here," said Mr Fudge shortly. "I had waited for a few runners to accompany me, but after that, I did not delay."

"What inspired your journey?" asked Judith, cautious and polite.

"My mother-in-law happened to make a comment about using this time to clean out some old things while everyone is occupied," said Mr Fudge. "And Jenny mentioned that the Beefsteak Club men seemed rather slovenly. Perhaps, she speculated, they were always leaving things about."

Judith did not look at Louisa-Margaretta, but she wondered about the two ladies. *Were they truly sitting about, in their fine gowns, making very innocent comments? Or had they considered aspects of the crime that had eluded Mr Fudge?*

"That was very fortunate," she said.

"Well, it would not have mattered had the two of you not been here," he insisted. "That was the most fortunate thing of all. I don't know how to thank you."

"Continue paying for your box for the entire run of performances," said Miss Byrd. "Perhaps convince some of your friends to do the same."

For the first time, Judith could feel her shoulders lowering, and all the ladies laughed.

JUDITH THOUGHT they would all leave right then. But before Mr Fudge followed his men, he approached her. "May I speak with you for a moment, Miss St Clair?"

Judith noticed one of the sources of Mr Fudge's power. Though he had overlooked many important elements of the case, he had not brazened through like a soldier. Rather, he was always gentle in his questioning. He had both an air of authority and a confidence that his authority would not be needed.

In spite of his weaknesses, she knew she would be a fool to underestimate him.

"I realised that I dismissed your concerns for Mr Ramsbury too quickly," he said. "I didn't think through the consequences of my statements, and I am very sorry to have spoken so harshly."

She stood straighter. "I hope I may say that I have never hidden from the truth, Mr Fudge."

He smiled wearily. "No indeed, Miss St Clair. You and your friend seem most determined to seek it out, a quality I would love to see more of in my men."

Then you ought to hire women, thought Judith, but she would never say such a thing to Mr Fudge. He might be prepared to offer his assistance, and if so, she was more than willing to take it.

"I have received word that a messenger is on his way," he said. "I don't like to trust to rumours, but I very much hope we shall have some good news shortly."

"And if we do not?"

He gave her a long look. "Either way, I'm determined to use all my influence to see to it that someone traces Mr Ramsbury's path. I lost my dear wife many years ago, and if I had not been able to mourn her properly, I cannot imagine how painful that would have been."

For a moment, Judith was unable to speak. Though she had fancied herself brave, willing to speak to Mr Fudge about any eventuality, she found herself hardly able to face him as he named her greatest fear. But she nodded.

"Farewell, Miss St Clair," he said. "Thank you for your assistance."

52

The mood in the streets was so jubilant that the wedding hardly registered with the crowd at first. But they began to notice that there was something particular about the joy of the few individuals who had attended. People alive with both excitement and exhaustion, seeing the first beautiful bride step out onto the church steps, shouted their congratulations. Judith wondered whether any of them would recognise the young woman's comely appearance from the stage of the Lyceum Theatre, but she imagined not. There was a great difference between a costume put on for professional purposes and the gown a young woman had saved for her wedding day. In spite of herself, Judith smiled.

Yet more cheers followed when the second bride stepped out. Judith applauded, the tears that were already filling her eyes threatening to spill over. She'd never been particularly sentimental about weddings, but her being was filled with both joy and sorrow. This bride was not as naturally beautiful at the first, but she looked every bit as lovely, so suffused was she with warmth and affection. Her groom's manner was solicitous and assured.

"A special license," breathed Miss Sweet. "Oh, Miss St Clair, did you really think we would be seeing two weddings this day? What better way to celebrate such a victory!"

The Duke of Ormonde had not been in attendance, but he was in the crowd, and Miss Sweet ran over to him to describe what they had seen.

Judith took out her handkerchief. Before she'd met Morgan Ramsbury, the idea of not having a wedding was something she relished. Marriage, to her, was an odd combination of duty and gamble. But she realised she could certainly marry someone like Mr Beecham, a husband who would be placid and kind. But without the wedding she had long desired, to the man who had captured her heart entirely, she was not willing to even entertain the idea.

"They'll be crushed in this crowd," said Louisa-Margaretta. "As will we shortly. Where is the carriage?"

Louisa-Margaretta was wearing a gown she could have worn to her own wedding, were it to take place. Instead, she was standing with Judith, looking relieved to have remained a spinster.

"Are your parents not angry?" asked Judith. "I thought after everything that had happened, well, they might not be pleased with either of us."

Louisa-Margaretta gave her friend a dazzling smile. "Well, Mama thought better of things, apparently. She hated the idea of seeing me unhappy in marriage, and my father was not quite disposed to approve of Mr Solier."

Judith took a moment to throw rice at the feet of Mrs and Mr Fudge, though to her, Mrs Fudge would always be Dorothy and nothing more. She was even Dorothy to Louisa-Margaretta, who had won her over by insisting that she use her influence with Mr Felton Fudge to convince Mr Christmas Fudge to get someone in the government to look into Morgan's whereabouts.

"I'm surprised at your father," said Judith. "Not that he disapproved but that this weighed so heavily with his wife."

"Oh, my mother only pretends to be in charge of everything," said Louisa-Margaretta loftily. "Papa almost never objects, but when he does, you can be sure he will get his way."

"And Mr Solier will leave London?"

Louisa-Margaretta nodded. "He is determined to go back to Paris. I have already asked the Duke of Ormonde and Mr Nightingale to take him after the opera has finished its run."

"And you?" asked Judith gently. "Where will you go?"

Louisa-Margaretta did not have a chance to answer, as Jasper and his bride were in front of them.

"Oh, my dear Judith," said the former Miss Wynn, "I am so pleased that we are now part of the same family."

"As am I," said Judith.

Louisa-Margaretta smiled. "Neither of you is quite so skilled at acting as I thought. All that business about pretending to be in love onstage! It turns out you just had to show your true feelings there then disguise them the rest of the time."

"Yes," said Jasper. "And now there will be no need for such subterfuge."

He squeezed his new bride's hand.

"You're not performing today, surely?" asked Judith, although she was not at all sure. Her experiences with actors had taught her that they always performed, no matter what was happening in their lives or the world outside. They reminded her of her father in that way, though the same could certainly not be said of every clergyman.

The new Mrs St Clair gave them a radiant smile. "No, not today. The performance was cancelled because of all of the celebrations. But Miss Byrd tells us that tickets are sold out for all of next week."

"That's wonderful news," said Judith.

Jasper gave a teasing smile. "They will all be hoping to see you, Miss Haddington. Even with all the victory celebrations, everyone is still speculating as to the identity of the bright young Alfonso from last week."

"I am very glad," said Louisa-Margaretta. "Mr Daw deserves a good crowd. You all do."

The Daws were outside the church, and Jasper and his new wife went over to them.

Louisa-Margaretta sighed. "I would like to go back to Derbyshire, to own the truth. I want to spend the autumn riding and hunting, not going to parties." She paused. "But you're not going to join me."

Judith's eyes filled with tears again. That time, they were not tears of happiness. "I long to see my family. Most dreadfully, in fact. But, Louisa-Margaretta, don't you see? I cannot leave London, not when I have finally found an ally. And if nobody can discover what has become of Morgan, I shall have to go to France myself."

"My French is improved," said Louisa-Margaretta stoutly. "You shouldn't have to go alone."

"Yes," said Judith gently. "But you do not wish to go to France."

Louisa-Margaretta laughed. "Of course I don't! A few months with a French fiancé have cured me of that desire forever, I think. Though I suppose I could be one of those ladies who goes and simply complains that it is not like England."

Judith's gaze had gone down the street, which was so full

of noise and revelers that the impression it gave was simply one of a crowd, not of individual faces. Interest in the double wedding had faded since the couples had been out of the church for some time.

But one figure at the end of the street caught Judith's attention. Louisa-Margaretta was still talking, saying something about France that Judith could not comprehend. Judith only gasped.

"What is it?" asked Louisa-Margaretta.

But the figure had moved out of sight. Even from the height of the church steps, Judith had lost him.

"Was that..." It would be madness to ask Louisa-Margaretta the question. She had not eaten enough that morning, or perhaps she was tired from the events of the past few days. There was no possible way she had seen him.

Then the crowd thinned a bit, and Louisa-Margaretta let out a gasp of her own. She left Judith's side, leaving the latter standing in her spot as if she were made of stone.

Judith could not think, could not speak, could not begin to comprehend the changes that a moment had wrought to her life and happiness. For Morgan Ramsbury stood before her.

TWO LADIES AND A MANHUNT

This is an excerpt, please click here to read the free ebook of Two Ladies and a Manhunt.

Louisa-Margaretta Haddington stood perfectly still, listening to a torrent of endearments and praise.

"Your beauty, Miss Haddington, can be compared only to the absolute perfection of your mind. You are the epitome of culture and grace, and I should not consider myself the least bit worthy of asking for your hand in marriage, were it not for one thing."

She could hear no more. "Really, I hardly think—"

"Hear me out. No man on earth could possibly be worthy of you, and since you must marry, I may as well ask. Why not choose me? For I certainly have several things to recommend me, though I would not propose to think myself your equal. For you are ever so divine—"

"Stop." Though she tried to look cross, she could not keep herself from laughing. "I am sure you are very wrong."

Louisa-Margaretta was tall, and though the praise for her beauty may have been exaggerated, it was still not far from the truth. Her tresses were reddish gold, her complexion radiant, her eyes lively. Her figure spoke to both perfect health and regular exercise, and all that was helped along by a surfeit of confidence. If Louisa-Margaretta had doubts, they were never about her own worth but only that of others.

Her friend Miss Lavinia Finch had been lying on the sofa, but she sat up and took a sip of tea. Though she had also been laughing as she professed her undying love for Louisa-Margaretta, she began to frown. After taking another lump of sugar, she stirred it into her tea. "Mr Fudge is far from stupid, in spite of his unfortunate name," she said. "You would be a fool not to consider his proposal."

Abandoning her tea, Louisa-Margaretta walked over to the pianoforte and began to play an etude. Though her technique was imperfect, she made up for it in the vivacity of her performance. "There has been no proposal," she said. "It would be improper before I am out."

Lavinia raised her eyebrows at her friend. "After tomorrow, you *will* be out."

Louisa-Margaretta sighed. "Yes, we shall both be out, I suppose. And I would rather die than be the next Mrs Fudge."

Glaring, Lavinia replied, "I am sure you would not wish to die, Louisa-Margaretta. There are many worse things than marrying an honourable man such as Mr Fudge."

Louisa-Margaretta switched to an aria, though she did not sing it. In truth, it was hard for her to imagine something worse than marrying Mr Christmas Fudge. He was twenty years older than her, not at all handsome, and a dear friend of both her parents. *At eighteen, am I to be a stepmother to his three children?* She could not bear even entertaining such an idea.

"You marry him, then," she said. "If you are willing to be Mrs Fudge, I shall wish you joy."

Lavinia was still glaring. "He has not offered any attentions to me, nor is he like to." And with that, she walked out of the room without a single word of goodbye.

"Did Lavinia leave so soon?" Louisa-Margaretta's mother asked, walking in and frowning at the tea things. "I wished to speak with her about tomorrow."

"Yes." Louisa-Margaretta had been answering Mama with only one word for days, and she was not going to give her any more information.

"Louisa-Margaretta." Mrs Haddington sat down next to her daughter. "I am sure that you may feel rather vexed, but ruining the reputation of our family is not the balm you are seeking. You must be polite to our callers, and tomorrow, you must put on your best smile at court. One does not snub the queen."

"Yes," said Louisa-Margaretta again. In truth, she had no quarrel with the queen, and she would not have any trouble with Mr Fudge if he did not insist on admiring her.

"Darling, if you will not listen to me, look to God for guidance."

"Yes," said Louisa-Margaretta again before escaping.

This is an excerpt, please click here to read the full ebook of <u>*Two Ladies and a Manhunt*</u>.

TWO LADIES AND A MANHUNT - 2

"These things are sent to try us," murmured Judith St Clair to her cousin Dorothy St Clair.

"It is not trying," said Dorothy. "Never, because I am not going to be defeated! I shall not accept it, Judith."

Tears of anger were streaking down her face. Judith, who was used to comforting people who grieved, found herself perplexed.

Of course, Judith's younger sister, Miriam, often cried over life's smaller trials. But ever since they had arrived in London for a visit, little Miriam had spent much of her time with their young cousin Rollo. At eleven, Miriam liked ribbons, but she was not interested in the talk of balls and coming out. She would rather run about with Dorothy's youngest brother, enjoying the sights of the city street from the window and getting paint on her best frock during their artistic endeavours.

"I am sure there are partners aplenty to be found outside of Almack's." Judith hated dancing and felt relieved that the most prestigious location in London was very far out of her reach.

"Not the sort of partner I would wish to marry," said Dorothy, sobbing again.

Judith tried a little pat on the shoulder then murmured some words of comfort before abandoning her cousin. If she kept trying to soothe her companion, she would likely say something that revealed her complete indifference.

When Judith sought solitude in her parents' room, her mother tried to rise from the bed. "I am sorry, dear," she said. "I should have been the one to comfort Dorothy."

"Her mother should do it." Judith knew she should not grumble, but as she took her mother's hand, she felt both more petulant and more comfortable.

"One of us should," said Mrs St Clair. "But as none of us had any expectations from Almack's, it is hard to know exactly what to tell her."

Judith's mother had carried at least three children since Miriam's birth but given birth to none. She had passed the time when things seemed to go wrong. Still, Judith was anxious and chastised herself for upsetting her mother.

"What is it, dear?" asked her mama gently. "You can tell me, you know. You and your father have been tiptoeing about for months. Only Miriam tells me things now."

Judith swallowed. She wished she could have told her father, but even with his gentle nature, she was quite sure he would not understand.

"I don't wish to be out," she said. "Oh, Mama, I feel the same as I did last year. Must I accompany Dorothy to balls?"

Mama sighed. "Yes. You are nineteen now, Judith. And your cousin is depending on you."

Judith turned away. She refused to argue more, but she could not imagine throwing herself into the world that Dorothy seemed to take for granted. The harsh conversations about wealth, birth, and childbearing prospects that she had heard her whole life seemed entirely apart from what she wished. It all seemed so very unholy. *How can my parents, who raised me to love and respect God and my fellow man, go in for such a thing?*

"Mama," she said.

But her mother shook her head. "You must be kind to Dorothy. She's had a very trying year, watching all her brothers and sisters leave."

Judith left the room. Of course Dorothy had been going through a trying time, but it didn't follow that Judith must be thrown into a marriage market so merciless that it was sure to make her own year equally trying. At least, she hoped not.

This is an excerpt, please click here to read the full ebook of <u>*Two Ladies and a Manhunt*</u>.

TWO LADIES AND A MANHUNT - 3

"Lou, you must be kind to Christmas, now," said her father. "He's had a trying year."

The Haddingtons were all gathered in their sitting room, as they had gotten word that Mr Fudge was going to call. Mr and Mrs Haddington as well as their son Sherborne were happily anticipating the visit.

"I have had a trying year myself," said Louisa-Margaretta. Perhaps it was not fair, but she found herself being gentle with her father, though he had the same annoying demands as Mama. "Why is there no sympathy for the sort of year I have had? Dragged to London for the season, deprived of my horses, forced to parade about in all sorts of silly clothing."

Papa only laughed. "Very silly," he agreed, chortling. "The hoops!"

Louisa-Margaretta saw her opening. Her father agreed that the ceremony of being presented at court was ridiculous. Perhaps she could enlist him, and they could talk Mama out of that particular requirement.

Mr Fudge's voice put the idea out of her mind. He had

entered the room and was greeting everyone warmly. She had to stop herself from sticking her tongue out at him. For years, they had gotten on well, as her fondness for the hunt and for her brother's constant games of cricket had amused him. Now she could hardly bring herself to look at him.

"It is wonderful to see you, Christmas," said Mama. "I trust we may see a great deal of each other now that we are back in London." Their country house was not twenty miles outside the city, but Mama always talked about it as if it were worlds away.

"I very much hope so," he said. His voice was low and gentle. Mr Fudge was one of the few people whose manners never seemed to change or slip. He was always polite, never condescending.

"I was hoping to see you all at Almack's... perhaps the day after tomorrow?" Though he addressed the group, it was plain that Lousia-Margaretta's company was his greatest interest.

Louisa-Margaretta's father grinned. "No. I'm afraid not."

Mr Fudge drew in a breath, and for a moment, the attention was away from Louisa-Margaretta.

"Not again," said Mr Fudge mildly.

"Yes!" answered Papa, sounding delighted. "Every year, in fact."

Sherbourne, who hated dancing and avoided Almack's as a rule, looked extremely confused. "What is every year?"

"They don't let Papa go," said Louisa-Margaretta. "It's a way of punishing Mama for not marrying where those harpies thought she should."

"Louisa-Margaretta. Honestly, you know your father would rather not attend. And I, myself, would prefer to be in church. But because it is your season—"

"Keep Papa out?" asked Sherborne. Of all the

Haddington children, he looked most like his father. But his brown hair was thicker, his dark eyes more arrogant. He had always wanted to be his father's partner in business but much preferred London to Manchester. Though he liked to think he was just as practical as his father, who had grown up poor, he was a product of his comfortable upbringing.

Mr Fudge shook his head. "It really is unconscionable, the way they split up families. If you would like me to have a word?"

"They wouldn't listen to even a magistrate, my dear," said Mama. "And truly, we need to stay in favour for our Louisa-Margaretta's sake. Otherwise, I would consider having a word myself."

"Harpies," said Sherbourne, which earned him a hard look from both his parents. "What? I'm sure they don't even know everyone by sight. If I were to go with one of my poorest friends from Oxford but dress him up in expensive clothing and claim he was a cousin, I am quite sure they would admit us."

"The day after tomorrow sounds delightful," said Mama pointedly. "Sherbourne, I am sure you will join us in your father's place. As I mentioned, it is important for your sister."

Sherbourne looked mutinous, and Louisa-Margaretta was secretly delighted that two of her parents' children were cross with them at once. Augustus was the only other Haddington staying at the London home, but he was to be married in two weeks and spent many hours with his bride.

"I can't think of a worse place in London," he said. "Nothing good to eat or drink and the worst possible company." After a pause, he added, "Meaning no offence, I'm sure, Mr Fudge."

"None taken," said their visitor, sitting and smiling at them all.

Louisa-Margaretta tried to keep herself from groaning. She could hardly tell which thing she dreaded more, being presented at court or being forced into an evening of dancing with Mr Fudge.

This is an excerpt, please click here to read the free ebook of <u>*Two Ladies and a Manhunt*</u>.

TWO LADIES AND A MANHUNT - 4

Louisa-Margaretta and Lavinia shared a carriage. It had been arranged beforehand that their mothers would arrive separately, as the costumes the girls were wearing were so large as to make sharing the confined space impossible for more than two young ladies. And though Louisa-Margaretta had better friends, she had always gotten on well with Lavinia until the day before.

She was not one to apologise, but Lavinia did not share that characteristic.

"Louisa-Margaretta," she said, "I'm sorry I was cross with you yesterday."

Their carriage was admitted to the grounds of the palace, perhaps at the very moment when even the most confident young lady might start to feel some nerves at the idea of being in Queen Charlotte's presence.

"You still seem rather cross," said Louisa-Margaretta, not looking at her friend.

"Yes, well, these circumstances would be trying for a better woman," said Lavinia, a pained look on her face.

Louisa-Margaretta examined her own costume and sighed. The hoops were large, the fabric distinctly uncomfortable. White crepe with a good deal of lace and ornamentation, it was the sort of garment that begged for a stain. She wondered when she was going to be able to eat another meal.

"These hoops shouldn't be so large," she murmured, trying to push hers into a better shape. "I feel ridiculous."

"We're fortunate they are," said Lavinia darkly. "We can all look equally ridiculous. Lord, what a silly show."

"Are you not happy to be seeing Queen Charlotte?" asked Louisa-Margaretta. Though she was dreading the spectacle, she would have thought her old friend might enjoy such a thing. Lavinia had always spoken of any brushes with royalty with great reverence.

"Perhaps I would be," she said tonelessly. "Tell me... What would you think if you knew this were the last time you would ever see this palace?"

Louisa-Margaretta had been distracted, thinking of how much time she would have to spend in the dull charade before she could beg her mother to leave, and the question sounded odd to her. "Lavinia, what do you mean?"

But the moment had passed. Lavinia was gazing out at the palace walls, waiting for the carriage to stop so she could step out. "Forget what I said. It is of no consequence."

Louisa-Margaretta frowned. "I wish you would tell me."

She would forget that conversation after, in the bustle of the presentation and her curiosity about the other men and women who were presented to Queen Charlotte. She had heard a rumour that the king was unwell, but they all had a chance to see him. And he did not look terribly indisposed as he cut a cake that was fully six feet tall, to the gasped admiration of the crowd.

She ought to have asked Lavinia what she meant. Later, she would have great cause to regret not doing so.

This is an excerpt, please click here to download the complete ebook of Two Ladies and a Manhunt.

TWO LADIES AND A MANHUNT - 5

Louisa-Margaretta had begged her mother to take her shopping. If she were to go dancing, at least she could wear the worst dress she could possibly find—something that would send a message to a suitor like Mr Fudge and would put him off her forever. At Queen Charlotte's ball the day before, he had hoped to dance with her, but she had retreated to a different room with what she claimed were nerves. Her mother had not been fooled, but unwilling to make a scene, Mrs Haddington had accepted the excuse. In the morning, she chastised her daughter, letting her know plainly that they would never go back to the country unless Louisa-Margaretta made an effort in London.

She could not have thought of any argument better suited to forcing her only daughter into compliance. Louisa-Margaretta, determined to dance, joined her mother in a dressmaker's shop while her father and brother went to call on an acquaintance.

"I think that black would suit me," Louisa-Margaretta said. "Something like this."

The garment she had found was a worsted day dress

made in a very deep grey. It might have done well for a widow, but she would be laughed out of a ballroom.

Mama was not fooled for an instant. "You are not wearing such a thing to Almack's. I don't know why we came. Look, there are Papa and Sherbourne waiting in the carriage. If this is what you had in mind for a purchase, we may as well go join them."

They left the shop empty-handed. Papa stepped out of the carriage and handed up his wife then followed Louisa-Margaretta back in after helping her up.

"I'm not sure why I must be forced to wear something in a gay colour," said Louisa-Margaretta as her mother began murmuring something to Papa about the horrid ball they were supposed to hold in her honour.

"White is a symbol of death in many countries," said Sherborne. "You could go in white muslin in a funereal sense."

Louisa-Margaretta pouted. "I shall be forced to go in white muslin," she said. "But I won't do any dancing."

A family passed their carriage. It consisted of a handsome woman, the roundness of her belly not quite perfectly concealed under a light gown and a coat, a pretty young daughter, and a plainer, dark-haired daughter about Louisa-Margaretta's age. Louisa-Margaretta smiled. So sour did the older daughter look as she was steered into the shop by her mother. They looked too poor to have to worry about Almack's, but the pressure for a good marriage was nearly universal for young women. As was the resistance to it, apparently.

Louisa-Margaretta looked over to see her father holding his head in his hands, her mother looking grim.

"Papa!" she said, shocked. Her father, as a rule, did not believe in illness.

"It's nothing," he managed, looking at her. "A headache."

"Anyone could get a headache from waiting in front of shops all day," said Sherborne. "Let's go home. We must all be fresh for the evening."

Though he had meant to tell a joke, Louisa-Margaretta could not help but agree.

This is an excerpt, please continue here for the free ebook of <u>*Two Ladies and a Manhunt*</u>.

Judith entered the shop with Miriam and her mother, as Dorothy had practically run ahead of them. Judith looked more closely at a dark-grey worsted, but Dorothy dragged her away.

"Don't be dull," she said. "That would never do for the season!"

"It would make a very good day dress," said Judith.

"Of course not. Oh, Judith! You would look ever so plain."

Judith looked to her mother for support, but Mrs St Clair looked very pale. She was touching the wall as if she would faint.

The dressmaker, likely taking note of her condition, found her a chair. "There you are, dearie. Don't try to get up too soon. Sarah!" she said, raising her voice without shouting. "Smelling salts for the lady!"

Mrs St Clair blinked. She usually hated when people fussed over her, even though the talk of her confinement made it more likely. But she settled into the chair and even sniffed the smelling salts twice. "Yes, thank you."

Dorothy, not at all concerned for her aunt, had found a beautiful dress in yellow silk. It would have looked terrible with Judith's thin dark hair but would probably flatter Dorothy.

"This one is lovely," she said, trying to pull Judith over.

"Dorothy," snapped Judith. "I must see to Mama."

"Judith." Her mother took her hand. "You are the most precious gift in the world to me and to Papa. Did you know that? You and Miriam."

It was a sentiment that Judith often heard from her mother, but rarely did a dressmaker's shop inspire such reflections. She frowned, wondering if Mama was feeling well and whether they ought to all leave at that instant to return home.

"Shall we go, Mama?" she asked.

"No, dear. Dorothy wanted to see the dresses. When she is content to leave, we must all walk back together."

Judith sighed. She was glad to hear her mother's voice returning to its usual vivacious pitch but felt that if she saw another series of lacy gowns, she would fall asleep from the tedium of boring luxuries that her family could not possibly afford.

This excerpt is almost over, please head here to read the free ebook of <u>Two Ladies and a Manhunt</u>.

"I shall never again wear lace," said Louisa-Margaretta. Her favourite fan had caught on her gown again, and as she tried to yank it free, she tore some of the lace.

Mama peered at it. "You will have to mend it yourself," she said, shaking her head. "If we were to return home now, we would miss half the dancing."

"I can't mend it. You know my skills with a needle go no further than holding it in my hand as I make conversation."

Mama sighed. "Your last two governesses were supposed to teach you, darling. For just such an occasion."

"Yes, well, they both failed to do so."

"Undoubtedly because their pupil was particularly unwilling to learn."

"Undoubtedly."

She gazed miserably over at Sherborne, who had been uncharacteristically gay the whole evening. It might have had something to do with the very well-dressed friend who had accompanied him. Louisa-Margaretta noted with a pang that her brother's friend was exceedingly handsome and wondered why they had not been introduced. Indeed, now that she had been presented at court, it would be proper for her to dance with such a young man, and she was surprised to find herself thrilled by the thought. For not only was he handsome, but he had something about him which drew and held her attention. It was the same, she realised, as happened at the theatre. Those who were most captivating on the stage did not always have the greatest beauty. But that young man, it appeared, had been gifted with both.

Without being told, Louisa-Margaretta covered the tear in the lace with her elbow. It might look frayed, but it was not large enough to attract undue attention in the crowded assembly room at Almack's. Besides, she knew that she had beauty enough that such a thing ought not to detract from it.

"Miss Haddington" came a voice before them, and she did not even think of suppressing a sigh as she turned.

"Christmas," her mother said, even more than her usual warmth flowing into her greeting.

"Mr Fudge." Louisa-Margaretta would not lie to him and say that she was pleased to see him.

"Miss Haddington. I trust you enjoyed yourself at court. Might I ask for the next two dances, if you are not otherwise engaged?"

"Yes," said Mama. "We have only just arrived. And I shall be delighted to see your very superior dancing."

"You are too kind. I know you would rather be elsewhere, but I am glad that you are playing chaperone to our dear Miss Haddington."

Mama's eyes sparkled. "How well you know me! Yes, my religious work is important to me, but so, too, are my dear children."

Louisa-Margaretta longed for a retort, but the music

finished, and she was forced to take her place with Mr Fudge.

At least he was a precise dancer and a silent one. Though he was not often in gay company, she noticed that he remembered all the steps and executed them well. Indeed, he had an excellent memory, something that she had often remarked upon when he was simply a friend of her parents who liked to visit their household. But ever since he had begun making sheep's eyes at her, conversation had been out of the question.

"How are you enjoying your season in London, Miss Haddington?" he asked eventually. "I hope you have been comfortable here."

"In the city?" she asked. "Never. I suppose the theatre is not the worst amusement, but if I were to leave London forever, I would have few regrets."

He smiled gently. "Where would you like to make your home, then?"

"I long to live in the country, where I can hunt and shoot to my heart's content. I would do almost anything to make this London season my last." Not that she would marry, of course. That was rather too steep a price to pay for the prospect of ending one's seasons. Besides, if she had a daughter, she would be forced back to London in sixteen years as a chaperone. Louisa-Margaretta, who hated the very thought of motherhood, saw such an eventuality as a rather cruel punishment.

"You do not wish for anything from your life apart from good hunting?" he asked.

Louisa-Margaretta, who had not had many conversations with Mr Fudge during the past year, could not tell whether he mocked her. But she did know that he was a kind listener, which meant she could be open with him in a way that she would not have dared with most gentlemen. "What else am I permitted to expect from life?" she asked. "A profession, for me, would mean the end of all social standing. So I am to live under the roof of my parents, brothers, or husband. It seems to me I ought to at least have a roof that does not leak."

There was little conversation after that, and it seemed that Mr Fudge was still blinking in surprise when she finally left him. She searched for Lavinia, hoping that she and her friend could at least take shelter while partaking of the rather disgusting refreshments.

But she encountered only her mother, who was also searching for Lavinia.

And the mission she had in mind was a much more dramatic one.

"Louisa-Margaretta," she said. "Think quickly. Have you seen Lavinia?"

The rumours were flying through the room already. Louisa-Margaretta saw person after person turn toward a partner, whispering with an intent look on their faces.

"She probably found it rather dull and went home."

Sherborne was standing with a man in a very fine set of clothes. Both of them were scanning the room, neither looking happy. Sherborne had pursed lips and pale skin, and his friend seemed to be almost swaying.

"Louisa-Margaretta," said Mama again, and she shook her head.

"You can call on her tomorrow, Mama," she said. "Is there anything decent to eat tonight? I suppose there is not, but I am very hungry."

Mrs Haddington was the mother of many children. The boys had come first, then Louisa-Margaretta, who was less obedient than any of her brothers. As such, it was rare for Mrs Haddington to become truly angry.

But there was fire in her voice when she spoke to her daughter again. "I do not ask for my own amusement," she said. Beneath the anger, Louisa-Margaretta was surprised to hear a note of fear.

"They found some of her things," said Mrs Haddington. "I am afraid it looks as if something may have happened to her. So I will not ask more than once. When did you see her?"

Underneath her mother's words, Louisa-Margaretta pieced together the story. She was not such an innocent as to be ignorant of the ugliness of the attacks that happened on women. *But not in Almack's, surely?*

"I have not seen her for ages. Just once, across the room, when we came in. But she cannot be far."

Sherborne had reached them. "We must leave," he said, his voice quavering.

Louisa-Margaretta noticed that his well-dressed friend seemed to have disappeared.

"Mama," he said. "They are calling in those Bow Street Runners. Please, let us leave."

Click here to read the free ebook of <u>Two Ladies and a Manhunt</u>.

9 781965 255285